Prisoners at the Kitchen Table

Polly Conover is showing Josh Blake her new fishing rod when a man and a woman stop their car and approach the two kids. They tell such a good story about being Polly's aunt and uncle, the ones that gave Polly a teddy bear when she was only two, that Polly is willing to believe they're her relatives. Besides, the man and woman say there's a nice surprise waiting at home for Polly. They invite Josh to come along too.

The next day when Josh wakes up in a secluded farmhouse miles from his home, he can't believe he didn't recognize that Bill and Verna were kidnappers. He remembers the policeman who came to his school to talk about safety—how he warned everyone not to get into cars with strangers. But the policeman never said kidnappers look like ordinary people, and pretend to be your aunt and uncle.

For one whole week, while their parents try to raise ransom money, Polly and Josh are forced to stay with tough-talking Bill and Verna, who watches television nonstop. It's scary and lonely and above all boring until finally Josh, who never thought of himself as brave, comes up with a daring plan for escape.

Barbara Holland

Weekly Reader Books presents

PRISONERS at the KITCHEN TABLE

Houghton Mifflin/Clarion Books/New York

For Matt and Ben

Library of Congress Cataloging in Publication Data
Holland, Barbara. Prisoners at the kitchen table.
SUMMARY: Two friends, one confident and the other timid, find
their positions reversed when they must plot to escape kidnappers.
[1. Kidnapping—Fiction. 2. Identity—Fiction] I. Title.
PZ7.H70815Pr [Fic] 79-11730 ISBN 0-395-28969-6

chapter one

Josh's mother came into the living room and said, "What in the world are you watching *now?*"

Josh looked up from the television. "I don't know the name of it, but it's really good. See those two guys? They aren't really people at all, they're kind of robots. They were sent from the planet Magda to—hey!"

His mother had clicked off the set. "You watched television the whole weekend. You were watching something last night. You can't come home from school and watch all afternoon too. Now go on outside and play."

"There's nothing to do outside."

"Go find the other kids and see what they're doing."

"All they ever play is dumb things like war. Last time Scott Breedon put mud in my hair."

"Well, ask them to play something else," she said. "Baseball or something."

He didn't tell her that nobody plays baseball in November. It wasn't the kind of thing mothers knew about.

"Look at that lovely sunshine. Go on, Josh."

He sighed deeply and went to get his jacket.

Outside, the air smelled bitter from people burning

leaves. Far away, from up toward the Breedons', kids were hollering, and a cap pistol cracked. Joey Ryan's voice called, "There he goes! There goes Danny! Get him, men!"

Josh Blake was small for his age, and not very fast at running. He really didn't like playing war. A person could get hurt. Besides, he was always the one that got taken prisoner. Or left behind to guard the fort and practically froze to death just sitting there.

It was a stupid game, anyway. Nobody ever lost or won. It just kept on going till dark or until some of the kids got mad or hurt and quit. Then the next day it started over again, with choosing up sides and building new forts.

He turned the other direction from the war game and walked down Locust Street.

He didn't stop to look back at his house. You don't stop to say good-bye to things if you think you're coming right back.

Mrs. Bell was cutting down dead plants in her flowerbed. She didn't see him, so he didn't have to say anything polite. Across the street, Mrs. Turner was pushing her baby in the stroller, and the baby was howling.

Josh's hands were already cold, even in his pockets, but it was too much trouble to go back for gloves. The wind came pouring up the street.

At the bottom of the hill there was a little stone bridge over Radley Creek. He decided to walk that far, then turn around and go back. Someone was leaning over the low stone wall of the bridge. As he got closer, he could see by the red hair that it was Polly Conover, and she seemed to be fishing.

It was a funny time of year to be fishing. Fishing was a spring thing, like baseball. Besides, there weren't any fish in Radley Creek.

"Hi," said Polly. "Look at my new fishing rod my dad gave me."

Josh didn't want to stand and talk. His nose and chin were frozen, and he was thinking about how warm it was at home, and about his television program, and maybe some cookies. But he looked at the rod politely.

"Watch," said Polly. "This is the kind you don't have to wind up by hand. It's got a spring in it, and you just push this thing and it winds up by itself. Watch." The line sucked itself in like spaghetti. There was nothing on the hook. "You can have my old rod," she said generously. "It just has an old baby wind-up reel."

Polly was famous in the neighborhood for having things. She always had everything she could possibly want, plus a lot of other things she hadn't gotten around to wanting yet. If you showed her something you got for Christmas, she already had one twice as big. She bragged that her dad would buy her anything she asked for, and it seemed to be true. This made some of the kids mad, but they asked her to play with them anyway.

It was a good thing to invite Polly to play. She had a catcher's mitt and a real wooden bat and a softball and a baseball. She had a leather football with laces, instead of the plastic balls everyone else had. She had guns for playing war, made of metal and wood and looking so real it was almost scary. She had a ten-speed bike, and the fanciest kind of skateboard, and real skis, and binoculars so expensive she wouldn't let anyone else hold them, even for one quick look.

Josh went over to Polly's house sometimes. When his

mother would let him, he liked to go at night. He used Polly's telescope.

He liked stars. It was a pretty good telescope for a little one, and he watched the orderly march of the constellations, staring at them until he could almost see the imaginery lines that hooked them together into pictures, the way there were in the book—the Great Bear and Cygnus the Swan and Pegasus the flying horse.

Polly cast her line back into the shallow dirty water of Radley Creek.

"There aren't any fish in there," said Josh. "They'd be dead."

Radley Creek was so polluted the kids weren't supposed to play in it in the summer, though a lot of them did anyway. Josh didn't. It had a kind of yellowy suds on it that looked pretty poisonous.

"Of course there aren't any fish, silly," said Polly. "I'm practicing. My dad might buy a boat. A real one, with an engine and beds in it. Maybe you can come with us sometime. At least, if my dad doesn't think you'd be chicken to come in a boat."

"I'm not chicken," said Josh, stamping his frozen feet to see if he could still feel them. "Just because I didn't want to ride that crazy pony. That's not chicken. That's sensible."

Last summer, Polly's dad was thinking he might buy her a pony, and Josh went along when they went to see one for sale. Polly rode it, and it jumped and ran around like a crazy maniac until Polly fell off and lay there on the ground laughing. Then Mr. Conover said Josh could try it too. Josh said no, thank you. Mr. Conover kept insisting, and Josh kept saying no, and finally Mr. Conover got angry.

The way it turned out, Mrs. Conover said a pony would be too much trouble, so Mr. Conover got Polly a tape recorder instead. But he didn't forget about Josh and the pony.

Probably he would never forget. Every time he saw Josh, he said something like, "Ah, there's our brave jockey," or "When's the big rodeo, cowboy?" Sometimes Josh had to scowl hard to keep from crying. If he cried, that would *really* give Mr. Conover something to be funny about. Polly never cried.

"I just think it's dumb to try to do dangerous things and get hurt," said Josh.

"How can you learn to do anything if you don't try?"

"I don't want to learn to ride ponies," said Josh. "A boat would be nice, though. Listen, I'm going home. I'm freezing."

A car started across the little bridge, and the man and woman in it looked out at Josh and Polly and slowed down. On the other side of the bridge they pulled over and stopped. The man and woman got out and came toward them.

"Hello there, Polly," said the man. "My, how you've grown since I saw you last."

Polly squinted at them through her red eyelashes. "Hello," she said doubtfully.

The man laughed. "You look like you don't remember us." He was short and plump, with hair combed sideways across a bald spot. "Don't tell me you've forgotten Uncle Bill and Aunt Verna!"

"I guess I have," said Polly. "I didn't even know I *had* an Uncle Bill and Aunt . . . what?"

"Verna," said the woman, who was wearing a shiny blue raincoat. She smiled at Polly and Josh.

"How do you like that," said the man. "And here we gave you that great big teddy bear for Christmas when you were just two years old. I bet you remember that teddy bear. With the blue ribbon around its neck? Big blue bow?"

"No," said Polly. She pushed the button on her reel and the line came swooping up out of the creek. A drippy plastic sandwich bag dangled from the sinker.

Josh thought she was being rude. You ought to at least pretend to remember people, especially people who gave you a Christmas present, even if you didn't see them very often.

"She was just a little thing," said Aunt Verna. "Way back then. Why, the teddy bear was bigger than she was!"

Polly studied first one face and then the other and shook her head. "I never even heard people talk about you," she said. "I mean, they talk about Aunt Nancy and how she got divorced, and Aunt Caroline and Uncle George. I never heard about you."

"Sure you have," said the man. "You just weren't paying attention. Of course they talk about us. It's just that—well, we live so far away."

"In Minnesota," said Aunt Verna.

"In Minnesota, and we don't get much chance to visit. We don't come east very often. Why, we were just talking to your mother, just a few minutes ago, and she was saying what a long time it's been since we saw you."

"My mother?" Polly frowned. "She's gone shopping."

"I know," said Aunt Verna. "She just now got back. She sent us out to find you and bring you home, so we can all have a nice visit together. She got something nice for you, too. That's why she couldn't come find you herself. She was fixing it up for you."

10

Polly's face brightened. "What is it?"

"It's a surprise. She told us not to tell. Come on, you'll see it as soon as we get home."

Polly took her fishing rod apart and fitted it into its case and followed them toward the car. As she was about to get in she stopped and said, "Listen, I'm not supposed to go in cars with strangers. I mean, even if you are my aunt and uncle, I don't remember you. I could walk home. I could meet you there."

Uncle Bill looked pleased. "Well, you *are* a good girl, Polly. That's right, that's very sensible. *Never* get in a car with strangers; it's very dangerous. But aunts and uncles, even if you don't remember them, aren't really strangers."

"Well . . ." Polly looked confused. "Are you *sure* you're my aunt and uncle?"

Josh was embarrassed for her. It sounded awful, talking to grown-ups like that, as if they didn't know who they were.

But Uncle Bill laughed and said, "Of course we're sure!"

Aunt Verna looked hurt. "I was so sure you'd remember us," she said sadly. "Your mother was sure too. And here we brought you a present, clear from Minnesota." She looked as if she might cry.

"Oh," said Polly. "Well, okay. Okay. I guess it's all right." She climbed into the car and leaned back out the door to call, "See you, Josh. Come on over later, and you can have my old fishing rod."

"Wait a minute," said Uncle Bill. He spoke quietly to Aunt Verna, and she chewed on her lip and nodded. "Hey there, Josh," he said. "We better give you a ride home too."

"No, thanks," said Josh. "It's okay. I can walk."

"Mighty cold," said Aunt Verna, and smiled at him. "I bet your toes are cold."

They were. The bright pale sky had clouded over completely, and skitters of leaves blew across the road. Josh's nose was starting to run, and he didn't have a Kleenex.

"Come on, come on," said Uncle Bill impatiently. "Nice warm car. We'll have you home in no time. Hop in."

Josh was a person who pretty much did what he was told. It was a good way to keep out of trouble. He argued with his mother, of course, and sometimes with his father, but with other grown-ups, like teachers, if they said to do something, Josh just did it. It made life simpler.

Besides, he was freezing.

As he passed around the back of the car to get in, he wondered why they had a Maryland license plate, since Minnesota was where they came from, but he was too polite to ask.

chapter two

He slid into the back seat beside Polly.

In front of him, Uncle Bill's neck made a prickly bulge over the back of his collar. They started off down Locust Street.

"You can turn around down here," said Polly.

Uncle Bill didn't answer. He just kept on driving.

Polly said, "Hey, you missed the turn. That was the turn. Now you have to go clear on to Elm Street and go around the whole block."

Uncle Bill kept on driving. Aunt Verna's long yellow hair hung over the back of the seat.

They passed Elm Street. They were getting farther and farther from home.

Josh began to get worried. The worry spread over him from the middle of his stomach and crept out to his hands and feet and made them feel bristly inside. Probably Polly and her dad were right, probably he *was* chicken. Because there wasn't anything, really, to worry about. It was just the way they weren't answering that made him nervous.

He leaned forward over his hollow stomach and said, "Listen, I can get out here. I can walk from here. It's close to my house." His voice squeaked. "I just remembered something I have to do."

"This isn't the way home," said Polly. "You said we were going home. You're going the wrong way."

Uncle Bill drove faster, and they turned a corner going farther from home. The tires squealed.

"Slow down," said Aunt Verna. "You want to get stopped?"

"This isn't the right *way*," said Polly.

"That's okay," said Aunt Verna. "We're going for a little ride first. Get some ice cream."

"It's too cold for ice cream," said Polly.

Aunt Verna turned on the car radio—loud—and the car was full of noisy singing. Then she took out a cigarette and lit it.

Josh couldn't see Uncle Bill's face, just the bristles on the bulges of his neck and the bald patch on his head. The worried feeling was making him sick. He was afraid he might throw up.

"I don't want any ice cream," said Polly. "We have lots of ice cream at home. I just want to go home. You said you'd take us home."

They merged onto the highway, into traffic, and passed a sign saying "200 NORTH." They were doing sixty-five. There were no ice cream stores along here at all.

There wasn't really anything to worry about, Josh argued with himself. These weren't really strangers. They acted funny, and they were driving in the wrong direction, but after all, they were Polly's aunt and uncle.

Only maybe they weren't Polly's aunt and uncle. Maybe it was a lie.

"Listen," said Josh. "I'm sorry, but I think I'm going to throw up."

14

Uncle Bill said a bad word. It was a very bad word indeed, the worst. It hit Josh with a shock like being punched in the face.

He was suddenly sure, quite sure, that the Conovers didn't have any relatives who used that word. Not in front of kids, anyway. No real uncle of Polly's would say that, not even if Josh really did throw up in his car.

He looked at Polly, and her face looked strange. Spotty. She always had freckles, but most of the time they didn't show much. Now the skin between the freckles was a milky-green color that made them show up like spots.

She leaned forward and shouted, over the radio music, "I don't believe you're any relation to me at all! And if you don't take me home right this minute, I'm going to scream!"

Aunt Verna closed her window tightly, clear to the top, and turned the radio up louder.

Polly screamed. Her greeny color turned to red, and she screamed and screamed.

Cars were passing them, and they were passing other cars, but nobody in them even looked. Everyone had their windows closed against the cold and probably their own radios were playing. Nobody heard.

They went past brown fields and some cows and a little airport. There was no one to hear Polly. She kept screaming anyway, stopping only to take a deep breath, and then scream again, until her voice got hoarse and wavery. Josh scrunched down low in his seat.

"She's got to cut that out," shouted Uncle Bill. "I can't drive. It makes me nervous."

Aunt Verna stubbed her cigarette out in the ashtray and turned around. She reached over the back of the seat and slapped Polly.

15

She slapped her hard, with a crack you could hear over the music, knocking her head sideways. Polly sucked in her breath so hard she choked.

Aunt Verna turned around and fiddled with the dial of the radio again, past some commercials and news to a different music station.

Polly had her hands over her face, but Josh could see the bright red mark spreading up beyond her fingers. He swallowed hard to keep down the throwing-up feeling.

Nobody ever hit Polly Conover. Oh, there'd been a fight on the school bus once, but Polly had started it, and she was winning, too, and Danny Wiggins was crying by the time the driver stopped it and gave them both bus-slips to go see the principal.

Polly wasn't scared of anything, and she was strong, too, and could run faster and hit a ball farther than most of the boys in the class. Now she slumped back into the corner of the seat with a crumpled look, like a doll that somebody kicked out of the way.

Josh was more than worried now. He was scared. It was all terribly wrong. He wished it would all just stop happening. He wished he could turn it off. He wished this whole piece of what was happening would stop, or run backward to where they were standing on the bridge, and happen differently.

His insides felt shaky and watery, and he took short breaths to keep from throwing up.

The radio played country music that all sounded alike, on and on and on. The inside of the car was gray with Verna's smoke.

Josh thought himself back to the bridge over Radley Creek and tried to remember everything they all said. Uncle Bill. Aunt Verna. The teddy bear they gave Polly

16

for Christmas. It all sounded so real and true. He tried to believe it really was true. How could they have made it up about the teddy bear, and Polly's mother coming home from shopping? Grown-ups didn't tell lies, except silly ones about Santa Claus and the Tooth Fairy. They mostly just didn't need to lie as much as kids do.

Josh tried very hard to believe that Uncle Bill and Aunt Verna weren't lying, and everything was really all right.

He couldn't, though. It wasn't all right. It was all terribly wrong.

Uncle Bill pulled out into the left lane to pass a truck and some cars, and another truck.

"Take it easy," said Aunt Verna. "You get picked up, we're really up the creek."

Uncle Bill slowed down and got back over to the right again.

They seemed to be driving forever. Route 200 North poured itself around long curves and slow hills and went on as if it would never stop. Sometimes they passed factory smoke or exit signs or a shopping center, but after a while, as it started to get dark, the countryside got emptier.

Even if we could get out of the car, Josh thought, we'd never get back home. It's too far. We'd freeze to death or starve. It would take a year to walk that far.

He saw two hunters in a field, in puffy orange jackets, with shotguns and a dog. He saw a little lake with a rotting rowboat pulled up on its shore.

Aunt Verna took out a pack of gum and peeled a stick and put the wrapper in the ashtray with the cigarette butts. She turned around and held out the pack to Josh and Polly. "Here, want some?"

17

"No, thank you," said Josh, and his voice croaked. Polly just glared at her, like a mad cat crouching under a bed.

They crossed a river and kept going north. The fields were tan with cornstalks scattered over them. It got darker. Uncle Bill turned on the headlights.

Once he turned the radio dial to some news. The newsperson talked about the Middle East and food prices going up, and some workers going on strike and an accident in a mine in West Virginia. "Nothing yet," he said, and turned it back to the country music.

Polly slumped in her corner. Josh wished she would say something. She ought to ask these people what was happening. It was Polly who should ask, he thought. It was her aunt and uncle they'd said they were, not his. Besides, Josh mostly liked to let other people ask the questions, and Polly was a person who asked them.

Only she didn't. He couldn't see her face in the dark.

He would have to ask them himself, even if he got slapped for it. He would ask as soon as they got around the next long bend. No, not that soon. He would ask as soon as they got over the next hill. Or maybe not until they passed that twinkle of lights, way ahead on the left.

It was so dark now there wasn't much to see but headlights, and not many of those. Finally he cleared his throat and said, politely, "Hey, mister? Uncle Bill? Where are we going?"

Uncle Bill didn't answer.

"Please," said Josh. "What are you going to do with us?"

Aunt Verna said, "You behave yourselves and you'll be okay."

"Yes, but where are we going? It's dark. My mom's

18

going to worry. I want . . ." He was going to say, "I want to go home," but just thinking the word *home* made him choke.

Home. It sounded very warm and bright, and very far away. His mother would be getting dinner. She would be looking out the window at the dark and frowning, wondering where he was.

The car kept bulleting through the dark country, farther and farther north. Farther away.

"Please," said Josh. "Is it going to take very long? What are we going to do?"

"That depends," said Uncle Bill over his shoulder. "Depends on how much her folks want her back. Yours too, since we had to bring you along."

"Want us back?" Josh's voice came out in a mouse's squeak.

"Yeah." Aunt Verna turned around to explain. "This is a snatch. Oh, come on, *you* know. Don't look so dumb. Bill here and me just hang on to you kids for a while, till your folks get up some money for us. Then we send you on back home. Just don't try anything smart and you'll be okay. Her too."

"You mean *kidnapped?*" said Josh.

"Yeah, kidnapped. Just like in the newspapers." She turned back around and lit another cigarette.

"Where's the map?" asked Uncle Bill. "Road ought to be along here somewhere. Eight miles past the bypass." He slowed down and leaned over the steering wheel. "Can't see anything. There ought to be a sign. . . . Never mind, there it is."

They turned off Route 200 onto another smaller road where there were no headlights but their own. Tree trunks flipped past them. The car bounced and jolted

19

over potholes in the road, and Uncle Bill cursed quietly to himself. "They ought to do something about this road. Break an axle along here. And no signs, can't find anything."

"That's what we wanted, isn't it?" said Aunt Verna.

They came to a crossroads, got out a map, and turned on the overhead light to study it.

"Straight," said Aunt Verna. "We keep on straight."

In the light, Josh looked over at Polly to see what she thought. She didn't look back. Her eyes were staring blankly ahead, as if she could still feel Verna's slap, and in her lap her hands were clutching the fishing-rod case. He reached over to touch her foot with his to make her look at him, but she just pushed him away.

Verna snapped off the light and they lumbered on down the dark road.

Kidnapped.

The word had a sharp, snapping sound, like a trap. Still, kidnapped was better than killed, he told himself sensibly. If he behaved himself and didn't do anything crazy to make them mad, probably they wouldn't hurt him. Probably he'd go home again.

What was happening at home? They'd be worried. It was long past time for him to be home. Past time to feed his cat. He hoped someone else remembered to feed her.

He had found the little stripey cat last spring, and his mom said he could keep it if he'd take care of it himself. He always did. He bought her a flea collar with his allowance, and kept the Kitty Litter clean, and fed her every night.

Now she would be walking back and forth in the kitchen, looking up at his mom with little wondering meows.

His dad would be home already, and his brother Steve from football practice. They would have sent Steve out to look for him, and he'd be back, saying he couldn't find Josh. Maybe they'd called the police. Maybe the Conovers had too.

Only police weren't magic. Where would they even start to look with the whole dark world to look in?

Mrs. Conover would be having one of her terrible headaches, the way she did when things went wrong. Mr. Conover would be calling up people like the mayor, demanding that something be done. Mr. Conover knew important people.

The headlights opened out on a brown, windy field with paper-colored cornstalks blowing around it. There wasn't any real road, just tracks through the field. The headlights touched something white. They pulled up close to it, and it was a little house with a crooked porch. No yard or driveway, just a house sitting in a big field.

Even if Mr. Conover called the President of the United States, no rescuers could find them here.

"End of the line," said Uncle Bill.

"End of the *world*, it looks like. Imagine living here," said Aunt Verna, and shivered.

They got out, and pushed the seats back for Josh and Polly to get out.

The fresh air was stinging cold after the smoky car and burned in Josh's nose.

"Now you can scream all you want to, Polly Conover," said Uncle Bill. "Scream your head off."

"I'm not going to scream," said Polly fiercely, and Josh was glad to hear her sounding like herself again. "*You're* going to scream when my dad gets hold of you!"

"He'll have to find us first," said Uncle Bill.

21

The car lights made a hole of brightness in the windy dark, and all around them there was nothing else at all. It was as black as closing your eyes. Josh had never seen such dark, without even a smudge of redness in the sky. No streetlights, no cars, no house lights—just solid, thick dark.

Uncle Bill and Aunt Verna were taking things out of the trunk of the car, moving in the red glow of the tail-lights. Uncle Bill felt in his pockets for a key, and they went up the steps to the rickety porch. He put down the portable television he was carrying and opened the door.

"Come on, kids," he said, "In you go."

The house was even colder than the outside and smelled funny, like old closets.

Aunt Verna found the light switch, and the room leaped up at them.

There was a white enameled kitchen table with some kitchen chairs around it, and a stove and a sink and a little refrigerator along one wall. Beside the door was a sagging red couch. There were no rugs or pictures. The windows had no curtains, and the night made them shine like black mirrors. In the middle of the floor was a hole with an iron grating over it.

Dark through the doorway, Josh saw another room, but it looked empty. Stairs went up into more darkness.

"Where's the *heat?*" said Aunt Verna. "Didn't you ask them where the heat's at? I'm freezing." She turned on all the burners of the stove and rubbed her hands together over the blue gas flames.

"There's some kind of furnace down in the cellar," said Uncle Bill. "Hot air comes up through that grating in the floor. I'll go start it soon as I turn the car lights off. And make something to eat. I'm starving."

22

"Sit down, kids," said Aunt Verna.

"I won't," said Polly.

Josh sat down on the plastic seat of a kitchen chair, and it shot ice-coldness up through his pants.

Aunt Verna took two pizzas out of a bag of groceries she'd brought in and put them in the oven. She set the television on the table, plugged it in, and turned it on. The picture shivered for a minute and then settled into a commercial for tires.

Josh's teeth were chattering so hard he was afraid they would break. Polly was still standing in the middle of the floor. He could see her teeth chattering too, and her nose was red with the cold. From the cellar they could hear Uncle Bill banging at the furnace and cursing, and then a whooshing noise. A rush of heat came up through the hole in the floor, and the cobwebs in the grating streamed upwards in the hot air. You could smell dust burning.

After a while it got a little warmer, but they all ate with their coats on. They had pepperoni pizza on paper napkins, the four of them sitting around the table as if they were a proper family. Josh looked at Uncle Bill and Aunt Verna eating and thought, how can they *sit* with us like that? How could they tell us all those terrible lies and not be embarrassed? I'd be so ashamed and embarrassed, I'd die.

But Uncle Bill and Aunt Verna went on calmly eating, as if this was the ordinary way to live, and they always ate dinner at a table with kids they'd kidnapped.

Aunt Verna made them all a cup of instant coffee. "Warm you up," she said.

Josh tasted his. It was hot but bitter.

Polly said, "I want milk."

"Tough," said Aunt Verna, and drank Polly's coffee.

While they were eating, the television sat on the table chattering away. It was a comedy program, and the studio audience kept laughing and laughing, with a clattery sound like empty cans falling downstairs. Every time anybody said something, the audience laughed some more, so it was hard to figure out what was happening.

For dessert, Aunt Verna opened a package of cupcakes, and Uncle Bill opened a bottle of whiskey and had some with his cupcake.

Josh was still hungry. He closed his eyes against the television and tried to see his own dinner table, his own family eating. Only maybe they were too worried to have dinner.

The comedy program was finished, and after some commercials there was a variety show with singing and dancing.

When that was over, Uncle Bill went upstairs and brought down two skinny little mattresses, the kind they have at a summer camp, and dumped them on the floor.

"Kids can sleep here," he said, "and you and me take turns on the couch here. Keep an eye on them."

"Hey," said Josh politely. "I have to go to the bathroom. Is that okay?"

Uncle Bill and Aunt Verna seemed surprised, which was silly. After all, they'd been in the car for hours, and sitting here for hours, and everyone has to go once in a while.

"Me too," said Polly. "Where is it?"

"Upstairs," said Uncle Bill. "You want to go watch them?" he asked Aunt Verna.

"What for? What are they going to do, jump out the window?"

Uncle Bill looked at them hard. He had little light-brown eyes that looked at you very steadily without mov-

24

ing, as if you weren't looking back at him, or didn't matter, or as if you were just something like food on a plate and not a person. Josh had to look away, down at the floor.

"Okay," said Uncle Bill, and shrugged.

Upstairs was a tiny cold hall with a lightbulb in the ceiling. There was a bedroom on each side and a bathroom in between. It was a strange bathroom, all wood instead of tiles, as if it was just an ordinary room where somebody had stuck a toilet and a basin and a bathtub full of orange stains. There was a beetle in the tub. It scuttled down the drain-hole when they turned on the light.

Polly went first. When she came out, she whispered, "The window's pretty little, but maybe we could squeeze through."

"You go ahead," said Josh. "See how far you can run with your legs broken."

Back downstairs, they went to their mattresses. There were no pillows, but Aunt Verna found some moldy-smelling blankets in a box upstairs, and Josh and Polly lay down in their clothes and coats.

Uncle Bill went upstairs to bed. Aunt Verna watched a cop program where they chased people across the rooftops, and then turned off the television and went to lie down on the couch. Josh watched the smoke from her cigarette blowing upward over the hot-air grating. Finally she stubbed it out and turned off the light.

It was so dark Josh couldn't tell without blinking whether his eyes were open or shut. "Polly?" he whispered. "You okay?"

"No!" she snapped back. "I can't sleep without a pillow. And I'm hungry, and the floor's hard. I'm getting out of there. First thing in the morning."

"How?"

"Just go. I'd like to see them try and stop me!"

"But where can you go? You don't even know where we are. It's hundreds of miles."

"I don't care. I'm not staying here, and they can't make me."

Aunt Verna's voice came sleepily from the couch. "Shut up, you two. I've got to get some sleep. I'm beat."

The blankets were scratchy and smelly. The mattress was so thin the floor hurt through it. Aunt Verna's breathing got louder, and she started to snore.

Outside, suddenly, quite close, there was another noise. Josh stiffened. His hair prickled on his head. It sounded like a ghost.

He, personally, did not believe in ghosts, not really. They were scientifically impossible. But this really had to be one. Nothing else would make a noise like that.

"*Aaah-ooo. Aaah-oo.*"

If it wasn't a ghost, what was it?

Then, farther away, another thing answered it: "*Ooo-oo. Ooo-oo.*"

Owls. They were owls. Josh relaxed a little, one muscle at a time. Owls were just birds. He was a sensible person, he told himself. Too sensible to be scared of birds.

Outside, it was cold, with brown fields and darkness and woods and owls. Inside, he lay on the hard mattress, with Aunt Verna snoring, and he was kidnapped. Really kidnapped.

He had been taken prisoner, not in a war game, by kids pretending, but by real, grown-up crooks.

At home, his family would still be awake. Maybe talking to policemen. But he couldn't think about home or he might start crying.

After a long time, the owls sang him to sleep.

26

chapter three

Josh woke up late in bright sunshine.

Aunt Verna was sitting at the kitchen table drinking coffee and watching "The Today Show." The sunlight was hazy with dust. Josh lay still.

In the morning light, he decided that Aunt Verna was older than he'd thought yesterday. Almost as old as his mother, even if her hair was so yellow. She was still wearing the blue raincoat, and under the table she had kicked off her shoes and was rubbing her stockinged feet together. One stocking had a hole in the toe.

She took a puff of her cigarette, coughed, and drank some coffee.

It was strange, how she looked just like anybody. You always thought if you met a real-life crook, you'd know. You always knew on television. They looked like crooks and talked mean. But Aunt Verna looked just like a plain person, somebody you'd see in the supermarket or on a bus.

Uncle Bill looked ordinary too. He was kind of fat and losing his hair, like Scott Breedon's father. Like lots of people's fathers.

It wasn't fair, Josh thought. It was sneaky. When the policeman came to school to talk about safety and not getting in cars with strangers, Josh had thought, boy, that would be dumb. Imagine a kid so dumb he'd jump into a car with kidnappers.

The policeman never said they'd look like ordinary people and pretend to be somebody's aunt and uncle. He never said they'd smile and be friendly and say "I bet your toes are cold." He never said they might be smart. Smart enought to make up a story that anyone might believe, with teddy bears in it.

On the floor beside him Polly was still asleep, with her coat collar turned up.

Josh was hungry. Pizza doesn't make much of a dinner unless you eat an awful lot of it, and it felt like long past breakfast time.

What was today, anyway? Yesterday seemed years ago, but it had been a Wednesday. Today was Thursday.

He had a spelling test today. That was a funny feeling. It made him feel lost inside, to think of Mrs. Rogers passing out paper for the spelling test and his desk sitting there empty.

After school on Thursdays he had cub scouts. They were going to make an Indian village today, and everyone was supposed to bring in all the popsicle sticks they could find.

Josh had eleven on the table beside his bed, along with his neckerchief and ring.

In his bedroom the sun would be shining in, and there wouldn't be anyone in his bed. It would still be made up smooth from yesterday. His mother wouldn't look in to see if he was getting dressed. She'd know he wasn't there.

Josh blotted up a couple of tears on the shoulders of his brown jacket.

"The Today Show" was giving the weather. It was snowing in the Dakotas, and a cold wave was coming across the middle western states.

"Aunt Verna?" he asked. "Is it all right if I get up?"

She jumped, and spilled some coffee. She stared down at him. "What did you say?"

"I said, Aunt Verna, is it . . . ."

"I'm not your aunt."

"I know. But you said you were Polly's aunt."

"Well, I'm not. *Aunt*, for pete's sake!"

"But what am I supposed to call you?"

"Call me? Oh, I don't know. Just Verna, I guess."

"I'm not supposed to call grown-ups Verna, or whatever their name is. It's not polite."

Verna squinted down at him through the smoke with her head on one side. "You know what?" she said. "You're weird. You are really one weird kid."

Josh was hurt. What was so weird about being polite? Or maybe what she meant was, if somebody kidnaps you and holds you prisoner, you aren't expected to be polite. Maybe she was right. "Can I get up?" he asked again.

Polly sat up suddenly, wide awake. She rubbed her red hair until it stood up like a bush and stared around at the strange room. "Hey, what's the matter?" she said crossly. "What's going on?"

She looked at Josh, and he could see her face starting to remember everyting. "*Oh,*" she said, and scrambled out from under the blankets and stood up. She looked ready to run right out the door.

"Take it easy," said Verna. "You better just sit down and take it easy."

"I'm getting out of here," said Polly.

"That's what you think," said Verna. "*Siddown*, I said.

That's better. Okay, you kids want some breakfast?"

"Toast, please," said Josh quickly. He was afraid Polly was going to get them both in trouble. "And some orange juice. If there is any, I mean."

"There isn't." Verna got out a loaf of bread and a jar of peanut butter and put them on the table in front of the television. "There's no toaster, either."

"Peanut butter?" said Polly. "For *breakfast?*"

"You don't have to eat it," said Verna, and spooned some more instant coffee into her cup.

Quietly Josh made himself two peanut butter sandwiches. They were hard to swallow without something to drink, but he was hungry. Polly sat and glared at the stuff for a while, and then made one for herself.

Chewing, Josh looked at the peanut butter jar and the bread. They'd had those in the car. They'd bought them somewhere and put them in the car, with the pizza and coffee and stuff, to have them ready so they wouldn't have to stop anywhere. They'd had everything planned out before they ever got to the bridge at Radley Creek. It made him feel helpless, to think how he and Polly were caught in a careful, complicated plan.

Verna switched channels, and a game show was coming on. The studio audience was yelling and cheering so hard the announcer couldn't get the show started. He kept holding up his hand for quiet, but they kept cheering. You couldn't tell why.

Bill came downstairs in his pants and undershirt. "Will you shut up that racket?" he said. "Can't you turn that thing off?"

She turned it down a little. "You want some coffee?" she asked, but she didn't get up to make any.

Bill made some himself and drank it, making awful

30

faces. "Stuff's lousy," he said. "Okay, listen. I've got to get some place where there's a phone booth, and do the calling."

"What're you going to ask for?" asked Verna. They both looked at Josh and Polly as if they were something they were wondering whether or not to buy. Josh wiggled uncomfortably and looked away from Bill's cool, steady, considering eyes. "We didn't talk about that. How much you figure we can get?"

"I thought maybe fifty thousand for the girl," said Bill, still looking at them.

"More," said Verna. "You saw where they live. Just their house alone's worth more than fifty, and he can probably borrow that much again from the bank. Make it a hundred."

Bill clapped his hand on Polly's shoulder, and she knocked it away. "Think your daddy can scratch up a hundred thousand dollars?" he asked.

She scowled. "My dad's got plenty of money. But he's not giving *you* any."

"My dad doesn't," said Josh hastily. "Have plenty of money. We don't even own our own house, Uncle . . . I mean, Bill. We have a mortgage. We have to keep paying the bank for it. The car, too."

Verna stuck her finger in the peanut butter, licked it, and said, "They'll scrape up something. People can always get some money together when they need it. What's your phone number?"

Josh told them, and Bill wrote it down.

"Better get some more food, too," said Verna. "Get some more pizza or something, if we're going to be here a while."

Polly jumped up. "*I'm* not going to be here," she said.

31

Her face was almost as red as her hair, and her eyes looked very blue. She didn't look scared at all, just mad. "And don't bother about calling my dad, either. I'm getting out of here and I'm going home!"

Verna made a dive to grab her, but Polly was too quick. She raced across the room and jerked the door open and was out before Bill could put his coffee down.

Verna scrambled up and her chair fell over. "Hey, get her!"

Bill yanked his suit coat on over his undershirt. "Hang onto the other one," he called over his shoulder, and ran out. Cold air poured in the open door.

Verna had Josh by the sleeve of his coat, and she was bending his arm so it hurt.

He wanted to explain that he wasn't like Polly. He wasn't the kind of person who would try to run. It was hard to explain, though, without sounding chicken, and he didn't want Verna laughing at him like Mr. Conover.

"Please," he said. "You're hurting my arm."

"Just don't try anything funny," said Verna, and let go.

Josh heard the car start. From the window, he saw Polly in her green jacket running and running and running across the brown field in the sunshine.

She was running as hard as she could. Josh could feel how the cold air was hurting in her chest and how the ground was lumpy and rough with cornstalks. How she didn't seem to go anywhere. She stayed in the same big field, like a painted person in a picture, running.

Polly was brave. Watching her, Josh felt a little jealous, the way you might feel jealous of how birds can fly. He could never be like that. He didn't even want to be, really. But still, it must feel nice to be brave and to pick up your courage and run with it like that. It might feel kind of like flying.

Now he could see the car. Bill was driving after her straight across the cornfield, and the car lurched and wallowed over the rough ground. Josh's heart started to bang. She couldn't get away from him. He wouldn't *run over* her, though, would he? Would he?

Polly tripped in the cornstalks and fell sprawling on the ground.

The car stopped with a lurch, and Bill jumped out.

Beside him, Verna said, "Got her," and unwrapped a piece of gum. "That was dumb, you know? Plain dumb."

Bill was dragging Polly by the back of her jacket, back to the car.

On the game show, a lady had just won a gold-and-diamond watch, and the studio audience cheered and cheered.

The announcer held up his hand and said, "Now let's get ON with the GAME! Our next contestant, a pretty little lady all the way from—where you from, honey?"

The lady whispered, "Seattle, Washington," and giggled.

"SEATTLE, WASHINGTON!" shouted the announcer. The audience cheered.

Bill pulled Polly into the house and kicked the door shut behind her. "You go sit at the table," he said. "And stay there, you hear? Next time you'll get hurt."

Polly's breath was coming in noisy gasps. She kept her face down in her collar and sat down on the other side of the television.

"Listen," said Bill to Verna. "I've got to go get the phoning done. Probably twenty miles to the nearest phone. You think they'll give you any trouble? We could stick them upstairs in the bedroom. The door's got a lock."

"It's okay," said Verna. "They're just kids, for pete's sake. It's cold up there, too."

"Here, I know what." Bill went back outside.

The lady from Seattle, Washington, won a vacation for two in Hawaii, and she was so happy she laughed and cried both at once. The audience whistled and stamped.

Bill came back.

He was carrying a gun.

Polly's head snapped up. Josh stared at the gun.

It wasn't a pistol or a revolver or any of those indoor guns crooks use on television. It was a hunter's gun, a huge double-barreled shotgun. It looked almost too big for the room.

Josh couldn't move his eyes away or stop staring, like a rabbit staring at your car headlights on a dark road.

"You know how to use it," said Bill to Verna. "The safety's on. And be careful. Don't forget it's loaded."

Verna took it with both hands and laid it heavily across her lap.

Bill turned up the collar of his suit coat and went out. The car started up. On television, a lady sprayed antiperspirant on her wrist and said it stopped wetness longer.

The three of them sat around the table, and Verna leaned forward to change channels, stretching across the enormous gun on her lap.

34

chapter four

The gun made everything seem more real—and more dangerous.

Of course, Josh didn't think Verna was going to shoot them with it. People don't just shoot kids. But Polly might do something else brave and crazy, and Verna might get nervous.

You couldn't tell what grown-ups would do if you made them nervous. There might be an accident.

He watched Polly anxiously. Her eyes were stretched wide and very blue, but she was still brave. She said, "My dad's got a shotgun bigger than that. It's got gold stuff along the sides, too. He's going to take me hunting with him when I'm older."

Verna just looked at her as if she didn't like her much, and turned back to the television.

This was a show where you made a mystery phone call, and the contestants had to guess who was being called, which seemed stupid. The prize was 10,000 green stamps. The audience knew who it was and kept giggling. It turned out to be some famous television person Josh had never heard of.

Verna changed channels again and got up to make

some coffee. She propped the gun against the sink.

Outside the window the sky was blue and the field was brown, and nothing moved. No people, no cars. It was like a picture on the wall, painted to look like a window.

Polly picked at her fingernails and fidgeted.

On this show, if you knew the answer, you pushed a button and a machine lit up and buzzed. If you were right, bells rang. If you were wrong, it made an angry, alarm-clock noise. It went very fast. The announcer would shout, "Is Puccini an Italian dish made with spaghetti? You have *seven seconds!*" Buzzers and bells and alarms rang, and he cried, "You now have ONE THOUSAND DOLLARS!"

Verna sat back down and stood the shotgun on the floor, leaning against the table. The two round eyes of its barrels pointed at the ceiling. She blew on her coffee.

The announcer asked what position Willy Mays played.

"Center field," said Polly.

The contestants knew too and won a trip to Miami Beach to stay at a hotel.

Josh wished he was at school. School was boring sometimes, but you always knew what was going to happen next. First Reading, then Spelling, then, on Tuesday and Thursday, Gym. Art was Monday, Wednesday, and Friday.

Today was Thursday. Field hockey. Josh wasn't great at field hockey, and the gym teacher got pretty sarcastic about how slow he was, but it was better than being a prisoner and sitting at a table with a loaded gun standing there.

He didn't even know where he was. It was sad and dizzy-feeling, not even knowing what state you were in.

Astronauts must feel that way, not knowing what to call where they are. Josh studied the view from the window and thought it looked like Pennsylvania. Of course, it might be Delaware or New Jersey or even New York, but he decided to think of it as Pennsylvania, even if it wasn't, so he wouldn't feel so lost.

There was a commercial about stuff you put in the dryer so your clothes won't stick together, and another where a lady was mad because her pie crust wasn't as flaky as another lady's.

Then the news.

The President was going on vacation. The police had cracked open a drug ring and arrested seventy people. A train went off the rails near Boston, and six people were treated at a local hospital for minor injuries. The search continues for two children missing since yesterday from their homes in suburban Westdale, Maryland.

Westdale! Josh sat up straight. That's where I live, he thought. Westdale's on the news! And then he realized that he and Polly were the children missing.

It was strange to hear about yourself on the news. It was like being two people at once—the Josh Blake sitting here at the table, and another separate Josh Blake that the newsperson was talking about, who was him too. Like being twins.

"Josh Blake is about four feet six inches tall, and weighs about seventy pounds," she said. "He was last seen wearing blue jeans and a brown jacket."

Josh ran his hand down the sleeve of his old brown jacket, which was now famous. This is the jacket you heard about on the news, he thought. Josh Blake's famous brown jacket. The one with the gray paint on it from the time he painted his bike.

"State police have joined local police in a county-wide search for the missing youngsters," said the lady, and turned a page.

Josh wondered where they were looking. He thought of his mother and father and brother, and the Conovers, and armies of policemen, all peeking under the forsythia bushes and sticking their heads into trash cans and shining their flashlights into dark cellars and calling into empty garages. Calling the way he'd called for his little cat, the time she was gone two days.

He looked into the newsperson's eyes. Here I am, he thought. Hey, lady. Look. Here we are. *I* can see *you.*

She was talking about a governor vetoing a bill.

Josh looked out the window. There were the bumpy tracks they'd come down the night before. The tracks crossed the field and went up into the woods and disappeared over the hill. It would be nice to see a bunch of police cars come pouring into sight with their sirens all screaming and lights flashing, coming to rescue them. They wouldn't, though. How could they? Bill had driven them so far, and cars don't leave footprints to follow.

Then a car did come into sight, and Josh's heart bucked like a horse before he saw it was only Bill, coming back.

The newsperson said that the school board would have to cut its budget.

Bill came in with a rush of cold air and set a bag of groceries on the table. The newsperson went on talking anyway, invisibly, behind the bag.

"You get hold of them?" asked Verna.

"Yeah, I got them. They were both home. Conover was kind of expecting a call. The other one, Blake, he thought the kid was just lost. Kept saying, why would

38

anyone want to kidnap *his* kid? Says he doesn't have any money."

"How long did you give them to get it?"

"A week. I said a week, and get it in small bills and leave it at the Sunoco station at the bypass from Route 200. I said, no funny business with the cops, or you'll never see the kids again."

"You mean you'd *keep* us?" cried Josh. "Forever?"

What a weird and horrible thought. Imagine living here with Bill and Verna for years and years. Until he grew up, maybe. Never going home to see his mother or his cat. Not going to school or even outdoors. Just sitting here until he grew up.

Or else that wasn't what they meant. He looked at the shotgun. But that was silly. You couldn't just shoot kids when you weren't even mad at them.

"Don't worry about it," said Verna kindly. "They'll get the money. People always do."

"Maybe the police'll find us first," said Polly. "And you'll go to jail."

"*You* keep quiet," said Verna. "You been trouble enough for one day." To Bill, she said, "You got some more food?"

Bill started pulling things out of the bag. "I got some more pizza. And coffee. And bread. I didn't know what else you wanted."

"You could of got some baloney or something. For sandwiches."

"Well, I got plenty of pizza. Different kinds. Cheese and sausage. And listen, we've got to take it easy on the money. We didn't bring too much, and we're staying here a week. We can't just keep buying stuff."

"We have to eat," said Verna. "And them too." She

stamped out her cigarette and went to put a pizza in the oven for lunch. "A week in this dump," she said. "You could of told them three days."

"Make sense. How'd they get it together in three days? They need some time. Talk to the bank, get a loan, sell the car. Mortgage. Whatever."

"We can't sell our car," said Josh. "We didn't pay for it yet. Besides, how would Dad get to work?"

"That's his worry, not mine," said Bill.

"Just the same," said Verna. "A week's a long time."

"Listen," said Bill. "We been planning this thing for months. This is the third try, right? We messed up on the Widmeyer kid, the one that hollered so we had to beat it. Said he never did have a teddy bear. We couldn't even *find* the other one, the one where his dad owned the trucking company. Now we've finally got one. One and a half." He looked at Josh with his cool, still little eyes. Josh scrunched down in his chair. He only counted for half, because the Blakes weren't rich. "For that kind of money, you can do anything for a week. Stand on your head for week. We aren't going to blow it just because you don't like the *house*."

"Go out of your mind here," said Verna, opening the oven to look at the pizza. "Ouch. This blasted stove!"

"I'm sick of pizza," said Polly.

"Nobody asked you."

"Couldn't we have hamburgers or something?"

"No."

Bill prowled over to the window and stood looking out and jingling the keys and pennies in his pocket. His suit was too tight, and bunched up across his back. "Keep thinking about the money, Vern," he said. "Think about maybe we'll go some place nice. Take a vacation."

The big gun was still leaning against the table. Josh could reach it if he tried. I could grab it up, he thought. Point it at them. Tell them to let us go. Take us home.

No. You could get hurt that way. Killed, even. That was a Polly kind of thing to do, dangerous and unsensible. Not something a little kid could manage. He had to sit tight and wait for his parents and Polly's to get the money.

Only suppose they couldn't? What happened then? Probably the Conovers could. They had plenty of money, enough to buy Polly a ten-speed and a telescope. But Josh was here by accident, just brought along so he wouldn't tell.

What *did* kidnappers do with kids their parents couldn't pay for?

If the Conovers could but not the Blakes, and Polly went back home, then Verna and Bill would be stuck with Josh.

This wasn't their house. They'd just rented it. Did they have a house of their own? Would they take him back home, if they had a home, in Minnesota or wherever, to be their kid?

He studied Verna at the stove and the back of Bill at the window. They didn't seem like kidpeople. You couldn't imagine them going to the zoo, or fixing a birthday party, or coming to school on parents' night. You couldn't even imagine them having a real place to live, a regular house with a washer and dryer, and Christmas-tree ornaments in the back of the closet. They weren't like that.

What in the world *would* people like Verna and Bill do with him, if his family couldn't pay to get him back?

chapter five

Friday was a lot like Thursday, except that Bill didn't go anywhere. He walked around the room, looked out the window, and went into the other, empty room, and they could hear his feet echoing around in there, and then he went upstairs and took a nap for a while.

The gun stood in the corner by the table, pointing at the ceiling, as if Verna and Bill had forgotten it. A couple of times Josh saw Polly looking at it in a thoughtful kind of way, and he desperately hoped she wouldn't do anything crazy.

They sat with Verna at the table and watched television. Sometimes they would stand up and stretch, and go to the bathroom, and come back. Outside, the shadow of the hill moved across the field and covered it, and then it was dark. For a while the only light in the room was the blue-gray flicker of the television, and then Bill turned on a light. They had sausage pizza for dinner.

Bill slept on the couch, and Verna slept upstairs.

The next day was Saturday, and they watched cartoons. Josh knew them all so well, and the commercials too, that he forgot where he was. He always watched the cartoons on Saturday mornings, and it made his mother furious. When *she* was his age, kids went outside and played games on Saturdays, instead of sitting by the television all day.

In the back of his mind, he kept expecting her to come in and tell him to go out and play. Finally, feeling guilty, he looked up.

There was Verna drinking coffee, and Polly picking at the enamel on the edge of the table, where it was chipped, and flaking it off with her fingernails. There was the crooked cupboard and the pizza boxes in the sink. The shotgun was standing in the corner, and Bill was drinking whiskey and staring out the window.

He wasn't home at all. He was here.

On Sunday, Verna didn't like the church programs and she put on her shiny blue raincoat and said she was going for a walk to get some air. Right after she went out, it started to rain and she came back.

In the afternoon, Bill said it was his turn with the television, and he watched two football games. It rained all afternoon. Polly said she didn't feel well and lay on the couch with her eyes open and looked at the ceiling.

Josh got pins and needles in his feet from sitting on the kitchen chair.

The roof leaked, and the bed upstairs got wet. So Bill slept on the floor downstairs, tossing and mumbling, and Verna slept on the couch.

Josh lay on his mattress and thought about food. He thought about fried chicken, mashed potatoes and gravy, and hamburgers with sour pickles on them. He thought about pancakes and bacon and eggs and apples. His stomach growled.

Monday the rain stopped, and the game shows came back on again.

Josh felt as if he'd been here for a hundred years.

It was getting hard to remember what his own house

looked like, or his teacher's face. When he closed his eyes, trying to remember, all he could see was the jiggle and flicker of television against the black of his eyelids.

They sat at the kitchen table.

"You're going to get cavities, chewing gum all the time," Polly told Verna.

"*Your're* going to get a fat lip," said Verna.

"Your teeth are going to fall out," said Polly. "Think what you're going to look like with your teeth all fallen out. Like this," and she sucked in her cheeks and lips to make her face look old and hollow, like a witch. She crossed her eyes. Polly could cross her eyes so hard they almost disappeared into her nose.

"Cut it out," said Verna. "That's disgusting."

"Maybe your hair'll fall out too," said Polly. "I bet it isn't even really blond. Is it?"

"None of your business."

"I bet it isn't." Polly was being as nasty as she could to Verna and Bill. Did she think they'd get sick of having her around and let her go home? No, probably it was just that there wasn't much else she could do. And if you had a personality like Polly's, you couldn't just wait and do nothing.

Josh hoped she wouldn't make them really mad.

The news came on and said that the Conovers and the Blakes were trying to raise the ransom money. The police had promised not to make any trouble so the children wouldn't get hurt.

The sun was shining.

"Verna?" said Josh. "Could I go outside? Just walk around the house or something?"

44

She squinted thoughtfully at him. "You'd try to run off."

"No, I wouldn't. Where would I run to?"

She shrugged. "That's the truth. Well, I don't see why not."

"No," said Bill, from over by the window. "Somebody might see him."

"Like who?" said Verna. "Some rabbit?"

"Helicopters. The police got helicopters, probably, out looking."

Outside the sky was empty and blue. Nobody, not even a hawk, seemed to be out looking for them.

"Nothing to see out there anyway," said Bill. "Besides, there's bears."

Josh thought that was a joke, so he gave a polite laugh.

"Sure, bears," said Bill. "At least, that's what the guy said that I rented the place from. I told him I wanted a place to do some hunting, and he said there was deer here, and bears."

"He was lying," said Verna. "There aren't any bears any more."

In the afternoon they watched soap operas.

A bunch of people were sitting in a waiting room in a hospital. A little girl with pigtails said, "But what if Mommy dies?" Then there were commercials, and then a pretty blond lady shot somebody in the back with a pistol, and he fell down dead. That looked as if it might be exciting, but it turned out she was only dreaming it or thinking about it.

It was hard to follow what was happening on the soap operas. As soon as you figured out what one bunch of people was talking about, it switched to some other people talking about something else. Or Verna got bored and changed channels.

Two doctors were eating lunch and arguing about the girl friend of one of them. Then it switched to the blond lady again, and she was telling two people she was glad they were getting married. She wasn't really glad, though. Later it turned out she was crazy and heard voices that weren't there, on top of dreaming she was shooting people.

"Can't you watch something else?" asked Bill.

"There's nothing else on."

"How can you stand that yammering all the time? It's driving me up the wall."

"What else am I supposed to do?" snapped Verna. "Go shopping? Visit the neighbors?"

"*I* don't know," said Bill. "I just wish you'd give the air a rest."

Josh smiled. Bill sounded just like his mother.

Verna changed channels, to the other soap opera, and said, "You want me to just keep walking around in circles, like you?"

Bill said several very bad words. He certainly knew a lot of them. Some of them Josh had never heard before and had to guess what they meant. He was trying to remember them all to tell Scott Breedon when he got home. Scott collected bad words the way some kids collect stamps, or empty beer cans.

If he ever got home.

"You shouldn't swear like that in front of the kids," said Verna.

Bill said some other bad words and went upstairs.

Polly went to lie down on the couch. Her face had that spotty, greeny look again.

46

"What's the matter with Polly?" asked Verna.

"I don't know," said Josh.

"Polly?" said Verna. "You okay?"

Polly wouldn't answer.

"Hey," said Josh. "Polly? Are you sick?"

She sat up suddenly and shouted, "Of course, I'm sick! If you really want to know, I've got diarrhea, that's what! And nobody even cares!" She bolted upstairs to the bathroom.

Verna raised her eyebrows and lit a cigarette. Josh was relieved. Diarrhea wasn't anything much, not like cancer or the things people got on the soap operas. Funny for Polly to get all upset about it.

There was a commercial where a lady was washing shirts for some man who must have been rubbing tar into his clothes. The lady didn't seem to mind. Josh could just imagine what his mother would say if his shirts looked like that.

Upstairs, the toilet flushed.

Outside the window the brown field stayed the same. Always, all day. Josh wished it would snow. It would be something different to look at. The only thing that changed was the shadow of the hill that moved as the day went by. And at night the constellations moved.

This was a good place for stars. At night when he lay on his mattress and couldn't sleep, and the owls were calling, he could look up through the window and see the Pleiades, near Perseus, and Mira, the variable star in Cetus, over to the east. It would be nice to have Polly's telescope here.

On television, a lady was talking to a man in a hospital bed. She kept saying she was carrying his child, but she wasn't carrying any child that Josh could see. Maybe she was nuts like the other one.

47

Polly came back downstairs and threw herself onto the couch.

"Boy!" she said, to the ceiling. "Are you ever going to be sorry if something happens to me."

Josh got up and went over to her. He was stiff from sitting still so long. "Diarrhea's nothing much," he said.

She did look pretty sick, though.

"It is too," she said. "Plenty of people die from diarrhea. If nobody takes them to a doctor." Her eyes filled up with tears and spilled over, and she rubbed them angrily out of her hair with the tail of her shirt.

She's *crying*, thought Josh. She's scared. Polly, who was brave as lions, was scared of having diarrhea, that nobody went to a doctor for because your mother cured it right away with that disgusting white medicine.

Suddenly he liked Polly a lot better. You could really like somebody if they weren't brave *all* the time. Besides, it made him feel braver to know Polly felt scared.

Bill came down. "I'm going out for a walk," he said. "Get away from that TV racket all the time." He glanced at the couch. "What's the matter with her?"

"She's got the runs," said Verna.

For the first time, Josh felt brave enough to speak up without anyone asking him. "I bet it's the food we're eating," he said. "Pizza all the time. It's not a balanced diet."

"Listen to the doctor here!" hooted Verna.

"I guess they didn't have it back when you were in fourth grade," said Josh. "We had it. You're supposed to have four servings of fruits and vegetables a day, and two of protein, and two from the dairy group."

"Dairy group, huh," grunted Bill. "Look, we don't have much money for food, and you kids are eating same as us. There's nothing wrong with pizza. It's good for you."

48

"Not all the time," said Josh. He was surprised at himself, arguing. Probably he'd get hit in a minute.

Verna said, "Get right down to it, I could use a hamburger myself. There's only one pizza left, anyway. We're out of coffee, too."

"We're out of *money!*" shouted Bill. He pushed his face up close to Verna's and said, "Can't you get it through your head? We're flat broke! I've got exactly ninety-four cents. Enough for one pack of cigarettes and a candy bar. Okay? Now let's just shut up about the food!"

Verna shoved him away and squeezed her cigarette pack. It was almost empty. "It's only Monday," she said. "If I don't get two packs a day, I start to throw fits."

"Tough!" said Bill. "I'm out of whiskey, and *I'm* not crying." He went to stand by the window and rattled the ninety-four cents in his pocket.

"We have to get some money," said Verna. "Some way."

"Yeah, sure. How? You want to put your tooth under the pillow? See if the Tooth Fairy leaves you a dime?"

"I always get a dollar," said Polly, still staring at the ceiling, "for my teeth."

"*You* keep quiet," said Bill. "There's only one way I know of to get a few bucks, enough to last us over till we get out of here. And we'd have to take the kids, too."

"Somebody'd see them," Verna objected.

"We wouldn't do it around here. We'd go a ways off—I've got enough gas. If we go on up across the state line and pull a job, and they see the kids and tell the cops, then that'll throw them off. They'll be looking for them up there."

"I don't think we should take them with us."

"We can't leave them here alone. And *you're* not staying here with them. I need somebody to drive."

49

Polly sat up. "Where are we going?"

"Nobody was talking to you," said Bill. She gave him her mad-cat glare.

Josh thought it didn't matter much wehre, as long as it was somewhere. He'd been sitting in this room so long it felt like a kind of suit he was wearing, instead of a room. It felt like clothes. If he bent his elbow, he expected to see the wall and the window crinkle up and bend with it.

Bill said, "If we just go up there and cruise the back roads, we'll find something. One of those dumb little country places where they've got one gas pump, and sell stuff like candy and cigarettes, and there's nobody for miles around. We don't need a crowd."

On television, two people were arguing about a girl their son wanted to marry, and whether she'd done something wrong.

"Okay, if you say so," said Verna. She lit a cigarette and peered into the pack to see what was left. "But I still don't think we ought to take the kids."

chapter six

The next morning, halfway through the game show called "Blackmail," Bill told them to get their coats on. They were going for a ride.

Verna stood buttoning up her blue raincoat, watching the show. Couples were supposed to tell embarrassing things about each other. One couple won a whole lot of suitcases.

"Shut it *off*," said Bill.

Josh gasped when the cold air hit him. He'd been inside so long he'd forgotten about weather.

They bumped along the dirt track across the field and up the hill into the woods. The sun was a dim yellow glow, toward the east because it was morning and south because it was November.

When they got to the highway they turned north. Old 200 North again, with the southerly sun behind them. The sun, and Westdale and their families, and his little cat and his own bed. All far back behind them and getting farther, mile after mile.

He hadn't thought there was so much north to the country. They must be almost to Canada.

Verna kept flapping a map around, trying to read it,

and folding it up all wrong. The big shotgun sat beside her, its barrel-end braced against the floor.

They drove over a ridge of mountains, and from the top you could see miles and miles of brownish-gray hills.

"It's nice you didn't want a crowd around," said Verna to Bill. "You couldn't raise a crowd around here if you took off all your clothes and hollered."

Polly said, "You better tell me what you're going to do. And don't think I'm going to help or anything. I'm sick."

Bill turned to Verna, and the bristly roll of fat on his neck bulged out over his collar. "Tell her to cut out whining," he said, "or I'll make her a lot sicker. Kids are a pain."

"You better explain," said Verna. "They've got to know."

"Okay, okay," said Bill. "Look. We're going to get some groceries, all right? Some food, and some money. Verna's going to stay in the car. You two come along with me, because it looks better like that when we go in. Just do what I say and keep your mouths shut. That means you, missy." He jerked his head over his shoulder at Polly. "We've heard enough out of you. Okay?"

"Okay," said Josh nervously.

"No," said Polly. "I'm sick." They ignored her. She stared sulkily out the window at miles of nothing.

Once they passed through a little town, but nothing was happening there except some dogs hanging around in the street, and somebody's wash out on a line, and then they were back in the country again.

Josh thought it didn't matter much where, as long as it was somewhere. He'd been sitting in this room so long it stuck with me. They'll take me around to help rob places—stores and gas stations and maybe houses. It would be a good deal for them. If people saw them with a kid, they wouldn't think they were crooks.

What a sad, peculiar life. Just traveling around the country looking for places to rob. No real house, no friends, no family, no school. Just traveling all the time, looking out the car window at nothing.

It made him feel empty and achy inside, just thinking about it.

After a long time they passed a sign that said, "Welcome to New York. Drive Carefully."

Josh always thought of New York as a city full of big buildings, but this was the state of New York, not the city. There was a bridge over a little river, and nothing else but hills and woods.

Verna had the map out again. "Turn off here," she said.

They went down a smaller road, past farms with cows, and through a town that had a car-wash place and a diner and two gas stations.

The road got narrow and bumpy. They got stuck behind a tractor for a long time, creeping along.

"My dad would pass it," said Polly.

Finally Verna said, "Hey, that looks good." Where their road crossed another road, there was a little store that needed painting. Its front porch sagged in the middle. Its sign said, "Larkin's Corners. Gas. Groceries. Soda. Cash 'n Carry."

There was an empty barn across from it with its roof half gone. A car was parked in front of the store, but there wasn't anything else for miles around.

Bill pulled over beside the barn and stopped. "Perfect," he said. "Give me that thing, the gun. You sure the safety's on?"

"Here," said Verna. "Better wait, though. There's someone in there."

"I'm not blind." Bill kept rubbing the roll of fat on the back of his neck. Josh could see little bubbles of sweat on it. "We look pretty silly, sitting here," Bill said.

"You're chicken, aren't you?" said Polly nastily.

"Shut up," said Verna.

They sat and waited with the engine running. Through the front window of the store they could see a lady in curlers talking to the storekeeper.

"Yak, yak, yak," said Bill.

Verna was chewing gum, her jaws moving steadily. "Don't forget my cigarettes," she said.

At last the lady in curlers came out, carrying a bag, and got in her car and drove away.

"Come on, you two," said Bill. "Remember, missy, you say anything, I'll crack you. Verna, keep the engine going. Honk if anyone drives up."

Josh got out and stood in the road on his shaky legs. His mouth was full of sour spit, as if he might throw up.

He had seen holdups on television a million times. But on television it was always the crooks who did it.

Now it was Josh doing it.

They never told you how it felt to be on the other side of the television screen, inside it. They didn't show you how scary it was to be the bad guy, with your heart thumping and banging in your chest until it made your jacket move.

He climbed the porch steps with Bill as if he weighed a thousand pounds, and Polly beside him, scowling. Bill carried the gun over his shoulder.

The store was dark and crowded with shelves and smelled of cheese and mothballs.

The storekeeper in his plaid shirt greeted them cheerily. "Morning, strangers. See you been out hunting. What can I do for you? If it's ammunition, I'm sold out. Won't get any more in till Friday."

"This is a stickup," said Bill, and pointed the big gun at him.

The storekeeper's mouth came open slowly. "Is this a . . . *joke?*" he asked hopefully.

"No. This isn't any joke. Put your hands up."

The storekeeper put up his hands. "Take what you want," he said. "I haven't got much, but help yourself. Only don't point that gun at me."

Bill went on pointing it. "Get away from the counter," he said. "You probably got a revolver under there. Back up. Keep backing. Stand over there."

The storekeeper moved backward with his hands up and his eyes on the gun. He stumbled over some sacks of dog food and fell back against the shelves.

"Okay, stay there," said Bill. To Josh, he said, "Here, here's a bag. Get some food. Get what you want. But hurry up!"

Josh still had the dazed feeling that he had somehow slipped inside a television program and couldn't climb back out. He stared at the shelves.

Polly picked up a box of cereal.

"You ought to be ashamed," said the storekeeper to Bill. "Bringing them. Nice way to raise your kids."

Polly dropped the cereal and cried out, "But don't you *know* us? It was on TV! We're the ones—"

"Stop that!" Bill swung the gun around. "You keep your mouth shut, or I swear I'll . . ."

He looked down the barrel of the gun at Polly. He was squinting through the sights, with his cool little pale brown eyes staring at her. The gun held steady. His eyes didn't move.

Polly folded up on herself and crouched down onto the floor. Her hands were pressed over her mouth. A thin whimpering sound, like a dog whining, leaked out from under them.

Bill swung the gun back around to the storekeeper and said over his shoulder to Josh, "Come on, hurry up. We can't hang around."

Josh began snatching at things on the shelves, hardly looking at what he took. Crackers. Some cans of stuff. It wasn't the kind of store that had meats and vegetables, but he found some milk and lunch meat in a refrigerator case. His hands were shaking.

What a way to do your grocery shopping, he thought, and he was so nervous he almost laughed.

Polly stayed crouched down like a kicked animal, her hands on her mouth.

Josh saw a shelf of things like Band-Aids and aspirin, found the awful gooey white medicine his mother gave him for diarrhea, and put it in his bag.

"That's enough," said Bill. "We've got to get out. Here, you," he said to the storekeeper. "Come open the register and hand it over. Don't try anything smart."

The register went *ding!* and popped open. The storekeeper scooped up the money. He was shaky and kept dropping things. Quarters and pennies went rolling and spinning on the floor. He handed Bill the money. It didn't look like much. "Sorry that's all," he mumbled, looking politely at the gun. "Saturday's my big day. Weekdays I don't do much."

Bill stuffed the money in his pocket. "And give me a

carton of Marlboros," he said, just as if he was a regular shopper.

He put the cigarettes in the bag and said, "I want your gun, too." He reached over the counter and felt around the shelf behind it. He pulled out a ball of string and a hammer and threw them on the floor, and then a bottle of whiskey, almost full, which he stuffed into the bag. There wasn't any revolver.

Then he grabbed Polly by the shoulder, pulled her up, and pushed her toward the door. He backed out still pointing the gun at the storekeeper. "Stay away from that phone," he said. "And stay back from the window. If I look around and see you looking out, writing down the license, I'll blow your head off. Got that? Just stand right still. Come on, you two."

Josh struggled with the bag, and they got out the door, across the porch, down the steps, and ran for the car. The bag was heavy. Polly stumbled on the road and almost fell. Bill ran beside them with the big gun, creaking and puffing, his meatiness jouncing up and down.

Verna had the car door open, and Bill yanked the seat back and gave Polly a shove inside that knocked her across the back seat and cracked her head on the window. Josh scrambled in after her with the bag.

Verna had the car moving before Bill was all the way inside. They were doing thirty by the time he slammed the door.

chapter seven

"**S**low *down*," said Bill. "That's all we need, the staties pick you up for speeding." He twisted around to look out the back window.

"We've got to get gas somewhere," said Verna. "We're low."

In the back seat, Polly whispered to Josh, "Listen, I have to go the bathroom."

She sounded ghostly. He looked at her, and she did look pale. Her freckled hands were picking at each other in her lap as if she didn't know what they were doing.

Bill pointing the gun at her must have rattled her up inside. It must have been spooky, looking at those two round eyes of the barrels staring at you, and Bill's awful little quiet eyes squinting over them. It was shuddery just to think about.

Poor Polly. Josh rummaged in the bag of groceries beside him. He found some cans of lima beans. Ugh. Whoever heard of lima beans in a can? Still, they were vegetables. He found the white medicine and passed it to Polly.

"But there isn't any spoon!" she wailed.

"Just drink some. My mom gives me a lot, maybe three or four big spoonfuls."

58

"You can't just *drink* medicine," she whimpered. "You have to *measure* it." She looked as if she might cry.

Cripes, thought Josh, she's cracking up. Polly the tiger, sitting there crying about a lousy bottle of medicine. It was weird.

He would have to take charge. "Polly Conover," he said, and made his voice sound very strong and grown-up. "You drink *exactly* four swallows of that stuff, right now this minute. Or I'll tell your *father* on you."

It worked. Polly opened the bottle and drank her four swallows down, gagging, with her blue eyes fixed humbly on Josh.

It made him feel about twenty years older.

"I still have to go to the bathroom," she whispered sadly.

"It'll work pretty soon," he said soothingly.

In the front, Bill was saying, "Thirteen stinking dollars. I can't believe it. *Thirteen dollars* and change."

"Maybe he was holding out on you," said Verna. "Is this where we turn?"

"Yeah, take a left. No, he wasn't holding out. He was so scared he must have wet his pants. Thirteen bucks. Drive pretty near a hundred miles for thirteen bucks. And no gun, either. That dum hick didn't even keep a gun."

"We got cigarettes, anyway," said Verna peacefully, blowing out a cloud of smoke that filled the car.

They stopped for gas. Polly used the ladies' room, and Josh got out of the smoky car for some air.

The gas station was on top of a hill; the wind blew, and all around you could see the brown tops of more hills and gray clouds. A German shepherd was chained to the side of the building. He growled when Josh went over to speak to him.

59

"You folks traveling far?" asked the gas station man. The wind fluttered his pants against his legs and blew the gasoline smell around in snatches.

"Yeah," said Bill. "Miami," said Verna, and laughed. Getting back in, Josh saw that she had spread part of her raincoat over the shotgun to cover it, but it stuck up in a strange way beside her.

Polly came out, still looking shaky, and got in and they drove on.

With the gray day, the smoke, and the steady sway of the car, Josh fell asleep. He didn't wake up until they hit the lumpy track through the cornfield to the little house.

"What?" he said loudly, staring around, confused.

"You were asleep," said Polly accusingly.

Boy, he thought. Pretty cool. Pull off a robbery and then just go to sleep. Joe Cool. He smiled at Polly, and she gave him a small, careful smile back.

"You feel better?" he asked like a father. She nodded.

Verna pulled up to the porch and switched off the engine. "Home sweet home," she said.

The room felt as if they'd never been away. Everything was the same. Messy mattresses on the floor. Trash in the sink.

Verna turned on the television before she took off her coat, and rummaged through Josh's bag of groceries. "You didn't get any bread."

"I was kind of in a hurry," said Josh.

Bill got out the storekeeper's bottle of whiskey and poured himself a drink, and a little one for Verna. She drank hers slowly, making faces as if it was nasty.

"Take it easy," Bill said. "You know how quick that stuff knocks you out." He went over to stand by the window where he always stood. "I guess the cops know what we look by now," he said. "And the car too. Won't do them any good, though. No way they can find us here."

He took a swallow of his drink and turned to Polly. "You've got a big mouth," he said. "You know that?"

Polly squeezed down small in her chair.

"You know what you need? You need a good spanking, that's what. And I've got a good mind to do it. Teach you to keep your mouth shut." He looked at her hard, and she went white in between her freckles.

"Why don't you leave her alone?" said Josh, scaring himself. "She's sick."

"You're getting mouthy too, huh?" He turned his little eyes on Josh.

Josh swallowed and said, "No. But she doesn't feel well."

"Huh!" Bill glared at him for another minute, then seemed to lose interest, and turned back to the window.

Josh let out a long breath. He felt as if he'd been in a fight and won.

It was dumb of Bill to be mad, anyway. It didn't make any difference what Polly said to the storekeeper. The police would know who they were. When the storekeeper told them, they'd know, from Polly's red hair and Josh's brown jacket, that Bill was the kidnapper. It wouldn't help the police *find* them, but they'd certainly know it was them.

It was silly to be mad at Polly, but then, Bill wasn't very smart.

Neither was Verna.

For the first time, he realized that you don't get smart just by being grown-up. You aren't any smarter than you ever were. Just older and bigger.

Bill was not much of a crook, even. If he was a good

crook, a smart crook, he'd drive a fancier car—a Cadillac
or a Lincoln—that smelled of leather like Mr. Conover's
car, instead of that heap out there that stank like an
ashtray.

He didn't even have a winter coat. Just that ratty old
suit that he turned up the collar of to keep warm. You
could almost feel sorry for the jerk. Probably he wasn't
smart enough for any regular job, so he had to be a crook,
and he was too dumb to make any money at that, either.

Whoever heard of a crook that's only got ninety-four
cents, so he goes and robs a little country store for thirteen dollars?

Verna wasn't any better. It wasn't smart to smoke all
those cigarettes, and she never knew *any* of the answers
on the game shows, not even easy ones like what river
goes through Washington, D.C. Then he remembered
what he was doing here, and stopped feeling superior.

Bill and Verna would be pretty rich when they got the
money from the Blakes and the Conovers. Unless somehow the police managed to catch them, they'd be doing
fine.

Somehow or other, they'd done one thing right. They
were smart enough to find a rich girl, and make up a
really good story about Minnesota and teddy bears, and
kidnap Josh and Polly.

chapter eight

For dinner, they had canned lima beans and lunch meat and cookies. It wasn't very good, but it was a change from pizza. Josh was so sick of pizza he could taste it just thinking about it.

It was Bill's turn to sleep upstairs, and Verna's to stay downstairs with the gun, guarding Josh and Polly.

Polly said she felt better, but Josh made her take some more medicine anyway.

She came down from the bathroom and said, "There isn't any more toilet paper."

Verna said one of Bill's bad words.

"It's not my fault," said Polly. "I couldn't help it. I was sick."

"I'm sick too," said Verna. "I'm sick of being stuck here in this dump."

"Wait'll you're stuck in jail," said Polly, but she said it in a whisper and Verna didn't hear. Then she went and lay down on her mattress with her back to them.

Josh and Verna stayed up watching a movie till one o'clock in the morning.

The movie was confusing, but Josh kept watching, hoping he could figure it out. First there was going to be a bank robbery, and then a kid set fire to some hay in a barn.

Then there was a commercial for the burning pain of hemorrhoids and one for freeze-dried coffee.

Then somebody came to town on an old-fashioned train. It was the sheriff, and he was the father of some people in jail. The barn burned down, and people rode around on horses and poured water on the barn. There was something strange about a set of door keys.

Then there was a mouthwash commercial.

Polly whimpered in her sleep, and flung her arm out, and her knuckles thumped on the floor, but she didn't wake up.

"Verna?" said Josh. "There's something I want to ask, if you won't get mad. How did you and him find out about us? About Polly, I mean, How did you know where to find her and who she was and all?"

Verna stared at him, surprised. "Getting real nosy, aren't you?"

"I want to know," he insisted. You couldn't be afraid of Verna, really, he thought. Not after you'd sat at this table with her practically forever.

"Huh. Well, I don't see why not. It's none of your business, but anyway last summer we got kind of broke. So Bill took a part-time job in a toy store in Baltimore. His job was putting stuff together—bikes and wagons and all—that come packed flat in boxes. Some people put it together themselves, but people with some money to throw around paid the extra, and Bill put it together."

So he did have a regular job once. It didn't sound like a very great job, though—not for a grown-up.

There was a commercial for microwave ovens, and Verna went on, her eyes flicking back and forth from

64

Josh to the television. "Polly's dad bought her a ten-speed bike. Real fancy. Bill put it together and brought it out, and Polly was there with him to try it before they took it home. Her dad called her Polly, and Bill just took notice of it, and her red hair. The last name and address were on the sales check, and he just copied it. All we had to do was drive around till we saw her. We got some other kids' names too, but it didn't work out with them."

So that was it. Simple. Even Bill could think of it.

"And she didn't remember him," Josh said. "Didn't remember she saw him before."

"Who's going to remember seeing people like that in a store? She was looking at the bike."

There was a commercial for car batteries, and then, in the movie, the keys turned up again, and the bank got robbed. People rode around on horses some more. It was the dark kind of movie where you can't quite see what's happening. Someone got shot—Josh couldn't tell who—but everything came out all right in the end.

The next day, Josh woke up late. He lay on the floor, looking up at the underside of the table, past Verna and out the window. It was snowing.

Sometimes the snow came down lazily, as if it was thinking about stopping, and sometimes it went spinning and whirling so fast it made his eyes ache.

He couldn't go out in it. He couldn't do anything except maybe go back to sleep. Polly was still asleep. There wasn't any reason to get up at all.

On the television, "The Today Show" was over and Verna was watching the one where they spin the wheel with numbers on it and people guess the letters that fill in a word.

That meant school had started already. The teacher

would be banging with her ruler to make the kids stop looking out at the snow. If it was snowing there.

It would be Reading. He had missed a whole chunk in the reading book by now. He wondered what page they were on. If he ever got back, they'd have to put him clear down in the lowest reading group with kids like Wendell Bush and Kelly Crisley who couldn't read *The Cat in the Hat*.

And think of the math he'd missed. His group was going to start fractions this week. He'd never catch up.

Somebody won a trip to Acapulco, wherever that was.

After Reading came Spelling. He was on the Blue Team in the spelling bees, and he was pretty good. Without him, they were probably losing to the Yellows.

After Spelling came Art, not Gym, because today was Wednesday.

Wednesday. He sat up.

This was the last day. Tomorrow was the day the Blakes and the Conovers would take the money to the Sunoco station.

If they had managed to get the money.

If they had it, they'd leave it at the Sunoco station, and Bill and Verna would pick it up. Then they'd let Josh and Polly go. Someone would come for them.

If the Blakes and Conovers had gotten the money.

But he couldn't think about that or what would happen if they hadn't.

Then home. His mom and dad, his little cat, and his brother Steve. Probably Steve would be so glad to see him that he'd ask him to play catch and let him use his chemistry set. His cat would sit on his lap and dig her claws into his knees and purr.

Scott Breedon would hang around, and all the kids would want to hear about it.

He'd sleep in his own bed.

Friday, he'd be back in school. Everyone would fight to sit with him at lunch and ask a million questions.

This was the last day of being a prisoner.

He got up and said good morning to Verna and went to get a glass of milk and some crackers.

The snow came spinning down.

"It's snowing," he said, to make conversation. He didn't say it was the last day, because that sounded rude, as if he was anxious to leave.

There wasn't much you could ever say to Verna. She didn't know much to talk about.

"It won't last long," she said. "They gave the weather. It's going to clear."

"Oh." He sat in the chair he always sat in, where the draft from the leaky window blew Verna's smoke in his face. Polly always sat on the other side, and Verna in the middle where she could see the television best.

Bill came downstairs, scratching his stomach with both hands, and made himself some coffee. "You're going to get cancer, watching that thing," he said.

"Huh?" said Verna, not looking around.

"Clean out your ears. Cancer. You get cancer watching TV all the time."

"That's just color," said Josh. "Just color sets give you cancer, if you sit too close."

"I heard where TV gives you cancer," said Bill, and looked hard at Josh until Josh looked away. "Anyway, it's giving *me* the creeps. Yammer, yammer, yammer. Those game shows are the worst. Eeek, I won a refrigerator! Squeal! Shriek! Bunch of nitwits."

He took his coffee and went over to stand by the window. Verna sighed and changed channels.

Polly got up and ate some crackers. "I can't drink that milk," she said.

"What's the matter with it?" asked Josh.

"It's horrible. It's blue. You got skim milk instead."

"I didn't look to see."

Polly kept giving Bill little nervous looks while she was eating, like a dog that thinks it might get kicked.

Today was the last day. Tomorrow they would be home.

The snow slowed down into separate slow flakes, and a little yellow sunshine showed through.

On television, two ladies were talking about a baby. It used to belong to one of them, and now the other one had it. The first one was sad. They kept looking down as if they could see a baby, but you couldn't. Maybe they just thought there was a baby. People on television got confused a lot.

Bill said, "I ought to go get some things. Some toilet paper. Pick up a newspaper and see if they got that money yet."

"You better not," said Verna. "You said yourself they've got a description out on the car."

"Yeah, well." Bill jingled coins in his pocket. "This place is worse than jail."

The morning dragged. Polly said she wanted to take a bath, she felt all itchy, but there weren't any towels so she didn't.

The sun melted the snow everywhere except in the shadow of the house.

A smily lady on television sang "Getting to Know

You" to a bunch of kids that looked nervous.

"Going to throw that thing out the window in a minute," said Bill.

"Keep your shirt on," said Verna. "It's the last day."

"Makes me jumpy, waiting. What if they bring the cops?"

"You told them they'd never see the kids again if they did."

"Maybe they didn't believe me."

There was a toothpaste commercial where a bratty little kid ran around showing everybody his mouth.

Josh poked his tongue around his teeth. He hadn't brushed them in a week.

Then it was noon and the news came on. The President was still on vacation. There was fighting in Africa. Trash collectors in New York were on strike, and there were mountains of trash in the streets.

Time was running out for the parents of the kidnapped Westdale children. They were close to the deadline and still had not managed to raise the ransom money demanded by the kidnappers.

Josh and Polly snapped up straight. Bill cursed and came over to watch, leaning across Verna's shoulder.

The newsperson vanished, and the picture showed Josh's house.

His own house. Exactly the way he'd left it—the front walk, the shutters, and the bushes under the window. A news reporter, who looked cold, was talking into a microphone. ". . . modest suburban home of Stanley and Eleanor Blake," he was saying.

And then there was his mother. His own mother, right in front of him. His heart pounded in his ears like footsteps running. She looked just like herself, in the shirt that was blue, only you couldn't tell on television, and she was upset.

The reporter pushed the microphone at her, and she said, "They were very kind and helpful at the bank. They did their best. Everyone's been very kind. But we just don't have anything to put up for a loan, or to sell. We've got some of the money. . . . We borrowed some from my husband's brother. We're still trying."

The reporter leaned over to say into the microphone, "And tomorrow's the deadline, is that right, Mrs. Blake?"

She nodded. "My husband's going to try to meet with them—the kidnappers. At the . . . place they arranged. Try to get some more time. He thinks we can raise it if we have another week."

"Another *week!*" Bill burst out, furious.

The reporter said, "And what about the Conovers?"

Josh's mother said, "They haven't got it either. Harold Conover makes good money, but they've always spent it all. He sold his car. They took a second mortage on the house. But it's not enough."

"Mrs. Blake, do you think the children are safe?"

Josh's mother turned her face away. "All we can do is hope so. He's a sensible boy, Josh. I'm sure he's being careful. I don't see how anyone could want to . . . hurt him."

And she started to cry.

Josh had never seen his mother cry before in all his life.

She got mad and yelled sometimes, but she wasn't a crying kind of person.

She was crying now. On television, in front of the whole world. Because of him.

The reporter thanked her and switched back to the central lady, who started right in on the weather as if nothing had happened.

70

chapter nine

His mother was crying. Not just tears in her eyes, but really crying, out loud like a little kid, because she was worried about Josh.

I've got to get out of here, he thought. I've got to go home and see her and say I'm okay. Right now.

Bill and Verna were shouting at each other.

"What do you mean, you won't?" said Verna. "You've got no choice that I can see!"

"What do you think we're going to do for money? Huh? Knock off another two-bit grocery store? Probably get five bucks the next time. Two bucks. Fifty cents."

"What else can we do?"

"I don't know, but we can't sit here another week. What are we going to eat? Leaves? I'm telling those deadbeats, get the money *now*, or else. And I mean it!"

"Or else *what?*" jeered Verna. "What are you going to do? Shoot the kids?" She waved at the gun and gave a clattery laugh.

Polly pushed her chair away and got up and backed against the wall. She was still nervous about the gun.

"I don't care *what* I do!" yelled Bill. "Except I know one thing, I'm not staying here. This place is making me crazy, and you with that damned TV all day!"

"Don't yell at me like that! What do you think—it's a picnic for *me*, sitting around here?"

Josh pressed his hands over his ears so he could think.

He had to go home. When he thought about his mother crying, he wanted to jump up and run and keep running till he got to her. But that was a crazy, Polly thing to think. Bill would just come out and grab him, the way he'd grabbed Polly. Or worse. Bill was nervous and upset now, and he might do something worse.

Just being brave was no use. You had to be smart, too, and think it out sensibly. Plan it as carefully as Bill and Verna had planned the kidnapping.

He wished he could get Polly alone somehow and talk it over with her. But she was too shaken up now to be much good. She was still backed up against the wall like a mouse in front of a cat, her eyes darting from Bill to Verna to the big gun.

The voices banged into his ears, right through his tight hands.

Verna was saying, "No, I won't turn it off, and don't you swear at me, either! The TV's company for me and I'm leaving it on. It keeps me from going nuts."

"It's *driving me* nuts!" Bill pushed past her and reached to turn it off.

Verna smacked his hand away. "Leave it on!"

Josh went upstairs to the bathroom where it was quieter, and looked out the window.

It was too high for jumping. They'd have to go out the regular door. Somehow.

There was the brown field and the hill. He was sick of looking at them. He could close his eyes and still see that view printed inside his head.

Somehow they'd have to get across the big, bare field, in plain sight, before they got to the woods.

It would have to be night.

They would go back the way the road went—east—over the hill and back toward Route 200. When they got to 200, they would have to stop a car. Explain that they were the kids that were kidnapped, and please take them to a police station.

The police would take care of them.

Only, suppose no car stopped? Or a car stopped, and Bill was inside?

No, he couldn't think that. Some kind person would stop and help.

The hardest part would be getting across the field without getting caught or run down with the car or shot at.

Getting out of the house would be tough, too. It was Bill's turn to sleep downstairs, and he was a light sleeper, tossing and mumbling all night, and sometimes saying things like "Whazzat?" or "Lemme alone!"

Josh would have to wake Polly without waking Bill. He hoped she wouldn't argue or bump into the furniture.

He pressed his forehead with his fists and stared down into the orange rust-stains in the tub. He had to plan it carefully. He had to be smarter than Bill and Verna. He had to keep remembering that they were just a couple of punks, that they had only had one clever idea in their lives, and that he was smart enough to escape.

He sat on the toilet lid for a long time, trying to think of everything that might happen and what to do if it did.

Up through the floorboards, Bill's and Verna's voices were still shouting.

"Because you're crazy, that's why!" That was Verna. "You go driving around in that car, and somebody's going to spot you!"

"I tell you I've got to get out of here and get a few minutes peace! Get away from that yammer, yammer all the time!"

Josh heard the door slam, the car start and thump across the field, and fade away.

He heard Verna's feet on the stairs. She banged on the door. "Hey. You dead in there or something?"

"Just a minute." He flushed the toilet, so she wouldn't know he'd just been making plans.

He would have to wait for dark. Waiting and not just running blindly off—that was the smart part.

Downstairs, the television was still going. Seeing it, Josh remembered his mother crying and had to tighten his teeth. Crying himself wouldn't help. He had to stay cool and sharp.

With Bill gone, Polly had come back to sit at her place at the table, picking her fingernails and glancing at the gun from time to time.

On television, two guys were arguing because one of them had left his wife, and now it turned out the other one was in love with her, and the first one was mad.

The spooky thing about television, Josh thought, was the way it kept on going, no matter what.

There it was, right in the same room with you, and it never noticed anything. You could ask it a question or scream at it or even drop right down dead in front of it, and it kept on going. You might be invisible, for all it cared.

Verna came back down from the bathroom. She seemed restless and prowled around the room like Bill. "Dumb jerk," she said to nobody.

There was a Pepsi commercial, with everyone excited and having a wonderful time and drinking Pepsi. They kept laughing and running around on a beach. They threw a Frisbee and drank some more Pepsi and ran into the water.

"I suppose he thinks it's some kind of party for *me*, stuck here," said Verna. She took the storekeeper's bottle of whiskey out of the cabinet and held it up.

There was plenty left. She dumped some cold coffee out of her cup and poured whiskey in it. She took a swallow and shuddered.

"Ugh! Horrible stuff. Nothing to mix it with even, like Coke or something. We don't even have any ice." And she sat down at the table.

"If it's so disgusting," said Polly, "why are you drinking it?"

"Only thing left to do," said Verna, and laughed her clattery laugh.

"Pretty stupid," said Polly. Verna ignored her.

On television, a bunch of people were talking about what to do with some kid named Bobby. Josh waited for Bobby to show up but he never did. People on television were always talking about kids that you never saw.

Bobby's father wanted to take him away from his mother, a silly-looking lady in a scarf, because she wasn't fit to take care of him. She cried and wanted to keep him. Nobody seemed to care where the kid himself wanted to be, but then Josh couldn't tell whether he was ten years old or only about two.

Verna drank her whiskey. There was a crack in her cup, brown from soaking up coffee. The whiskey smelled awful, and Verna shuddered with every swallow.

There was a commercial for a safe, gentle laxative.

Verna went back to the sink and poked gloomily

among the mess—the pizza wrappers, and cans, and the whole brown, smelly stew of cigarette butts. Verna was afraid of fires, so every night before she went to bed she dumped the ashtray into the sink and ran water over the mess.

"Might as well get drunk," she said, and poured some more whiskey.

The afternoon went on and on, and the shadow of the hill moved across the field.

"Whose idea was it, anyway, I'd like to know?" said Verna. She seemed to be asking the television. "It was his idea, that's who. Wasn't *my* idea." The television, naturally, paid no attention.

She got up and poured some more whiskey. "All *I* ever wanted," she said, "was maybe get a little place somewhere. Settle down."

Her voice sounded funny, and Josh pricked up his ears. She sounded mumbly and mushy, like people on television who got drunk.

When people got drunk, they got pretty stupid and tripped over things. If they weren't very smart to begin with, being drunk on top of it would mean they were too dumb to find their head with both hands.

Josh could feel his insides sharpening up, getting ready.

The shadow of the hill had already swallowed up the field. It got dark early this time of year.

Bill was still gone. He might be back any minute. Josh thought about his cold, steady little eyes and how they looked at you as if you didn't matter. His stomach clutched up nervously.

"Never even had a chance to cook anything, even," said Verna sadly. "My mother, she was a good cook. I could've been a good cook too, ever had any *place* to cook. Real kitchen. Place of my own. You get sick of just heating up frozen stuff all the time." She shook the bottle upside down for the last drops.

"All gone," she said. She set it down on the edge of the counter, and it tipped and fell and smashed on the floor. She stared down at the pieces. "Oopsy," she said.

Crunching bits of glass underfoot, she came back to the table. As she sat down, she bumped the big shotgun. Its barrel slid along the edge of the table and it crashed down onto the floor, pointing at Josh's foot. Verna didn't seem to notice.

Josh looked at it. He didn't like guns. He didn't even like *pretend* guns. On the other hand, if you were careful, it wasn't going to turn around in your hands and shoot you. Guns couldn't move. Even if you were just a kid, if you were smart, a gun you were holding yourself couldn't hurt you. It couldn't even hurt someone else unless you wanted it to.

Verna was laughing to herself. "Pretty funny. Get a little place and settle down. That's what I wanted. Well, that's what we did!" She waved her arm around at the room. "Got a little place. Settle down. Jeez, what a dump!" She stopped laughing and tossed her head back. "Be stuck here forever, prob'ly."

The dark came on quickly, and the blue light from the television was the only bright thing in the room.

Josh gathered himself carefully together. If only Bill stayed away, with his awful eyes and the car. The car with its headlights for spotting kids running.

Polly switched on the bright bare lightbulb in the ceiling and they all blinked in the sudden light. Verna's head was lolling back and forth as if her neck couldn't hold it straight.

On television, a lady was in a hospital bed, and her

husband was trying to talk to her, telling her he loved her, and all that glop. You couldn't see why he bothered, since she was out cold and not listening.

"Darling, speak to me," said the husband. "Darling, you've got so much to live for. Think of the children." And he started to sniffle, but the lady didn't budge. "We've had so many wonderful moments together," he said, and wiped his nose.

The doctor came in, held the lady's wrist, and then dropped it. "I'm sorry, Jim," he said to the husband.

"No! No! No!" said the husband, and cried harder.

Verna was crying too, sniffling up her tears.

If you were going to do something, there was a right time to do it. You had to snatch at the right time when it came—not wait around till it slipped past. You had to know the right time when you saw it.

Josh was nervous; he wanted to wait. But Bill might come back. This was the right time. Now. Not later in the night, the way he'd planned it, with the car here. Now.

He hooked the barrel of the big gun with his foot, pulled it closer, and bent over and picked it up. Very coolly. As if he was just putting it back where it belonged.

Verna was completely sunk in the program, and sniffling. Her mouth hung open.

Josh pushed his chair back and turned the gun around in the right direction. It was very heavy. He stood up and pointed it down at the floor to be safe.

"Please sit still right there, Verna," he said. "Don't get up or anything. I'm sorry, but my mom's worried. Polly and I have to go home."

chapter ten

Verna blinked at him, confused. "You better watch it," she said. "You better put that gun down. You don't even know how to use it."

"I do," said Polly, and jumped up. She darted past Verna, out of reach, and over to Josh. "My dad's got one just like it, only his is better." Her eyes were sharply blue and bright again as her courage came back to her, standing behind the gun now instead of in front of it.

"This is the safety, Josh, look," she said. "Like this it can't shoot. If you do it like this, it can. All you do is squeeze the trigger, and *bam!*"

"Get your jacket," said Josh. "Get mine too. We've got to go."

Polly poked her tongue out at Verna and gathered up their jackets. Josh backed toward the door clumsily, holding the gun pointed down. The television was talking about aspirin and faster relief from headache pain.

Verna seemed to understand now. Slowly, through the whiskey, she began to realize that he wasn't kidding. She stood up, hanging onto the table, and started unsteadily toward him.

"Cut it out," she said. "You better cut it out or you'll be sorry. You hear me?"

Josh was up against the door now. He couldn't possibly shoot at her. But he had to make her believe he would. "Back off," he said. He pointed the gun at her feet. "Go on," she said. "Polly took the safety off. Get back. I'll hurt you."

Verna stood still, weaving a little. "You're not going to shoot that thing," she said, but she didn't sound sure. "You're only a kid. Gimme the gun. Gimme that gun or I'll crack you one."

"No." He held it steady at her feet. "I won't. We have to go."

She frowned at the gun. Sober, she would just have taken it away from him. Drunk, she didn't seem to know what to do.

"Go sit down," said Josh. He was faking it, bossing her around, trying to talk tough. Scott Breedon or anyone would have laughed at him.

But Verna stood there swaying on her feet for a minute, frowning, uncertain, and then turned and made her way back to the table and sat down.

"You'll be sorry," she muttered. "It's dark. You're gonna get lost."

"Good-bye," said Josh.

She thought of something else. "What'll I say to Bill? What about Bill? He'll *kill* me."

"I'm sorry. Good-bye."

Polly opened the door behind him, and Josh backed out through it with the gun, tripping over the doorsill. Verna sat still.

The last they could hear was a shampoo commercial with girls singing that their hair was more than just clean.

Beyond the light from the doorway it was inky dark

and cold. Josh put the safety back on and laid the gun on the ground and struggled into the sleeves of his jacket. Then he picked the gun up again, and together they started out into the dark field, feeling their way ahead with their feet.

If Bill came back now, his headlights would pick them out as bright as day and throw their long shadows. There'd be no way to outrun his car chasing them.

Behind them the house was like a lighted box. When they had gone a little way, they looked back and saw Verna in the open doorway, holding onto its sides with both hands and leaning out, but she didn't call or come after them.

"How can we find the road?" asked Polly.

"We can't use the road. We have to go through the woods."

"In the *dark?*"

"Ow!" Josh missed his footing in the rough ground and nearly fell on the gun. "Bill's going to come back on the road. Any minute, probably. And there we'd be in the headlights.

"We could shoot him," said Polly.

"Are you crazy?"

"But how can we walk in the woods in the dark, with the rocks and prickers and everything? Besides, we won't know where we're going. My dad says, if you get lost, you just keep walking in circles. You have to just sit still and wait for someone to find you."

"Who? Bill? Slow down, this thing's heavy."

"We could freeze to death, or starve, just going in circles!"

"We *aren't* lost," said Josh. "Look, the highway's over there, Route 200, west of us, right? That's the direction we came from. It runs north and south and it's right across from us, so we can't miss hitting it, if we keep going west."

"But we don't know where west is."

Josh looked up. Overhead the stars hung in their places in the clear country air, familiar and friendly as his bedroom ceiling at home. "There's Polaris. The Pole Star. It points to the north. We just keep it over our right shoulders, like now."

"Oh yeah? How do you know it's the Pole Star? They all look the same. Suppose you're looking at the wrong star?"

Suppose he was? For a moment he was worried and saw the stars the way Polly did, as a big mess of little lights, like pinholes in a black lampshade. But that wasn't true. They had names, and they hung in their proper patterns, and you could trust them. The Vikings did, and found their way all over the ocean.

"There's the Little Bear, Ursa Minor," he said. "Can you see where I'm pointing?" He aimed the gun into the sky.

"No."

"You call it the Little Dipper. It's right over the Big Dipper. See?"

"No."

"Well, I can. Polaris is the tip of the Little Bear's tail. Come on."

"I don't believe you," said Polly in the dark, with spirit. "It's only in books people find their way around with stars. Indians and stuff. *You* can't."

"I can so," said Josh. "Besides, you've *got* to believe me. What else are you going to do?" And he laughed and felt strong and almost safe with Polaris to take care of him.

They had come to the edge of the woods now, and the trees stood up dark against the stars. He heard Polly stop and felt her turn to look back at the lighted box behind them, as if it looked safer than the dark woods. "I forgot my fishing rod," she said.

"Go on back then, if you want," said Josh. "I'm going home. I have to tell Mom I'm okay." He pushed into the scratchy tangle, holding the gun up to protect his face.

Polly came slowly after him, complaining of thorns.

Through the bare trees, Polaris burned steadily in the north where it belonged. There was no moon.

The big gun caught on a tree and punched Josh in the stomach. "Oof," he grunted. "Hey, I can't carry this thing here." He threw it awkwardly away from him, end over end, and heard it crash somewhere in leaves and bushes. He was glad he hadn't had to shoot it.

"What'd you do that for?" asked Polly's voice. "Those things cost a lot of money. You could've kept it."

"I don't want it." Now he had two free hands.

An owl hooted.

Behind him, Polly said, "That sounds scary."

"They're just birds," said Josh.

It was cold. A thin sharp wind came knifing in through their jackets. They hunched down and bent their heads against it. Without gloves, their hands ached with cold, but they couldn't put them in their pockets. They needed them to feel the way and push back branches.

Walking faster or running would have been warmer, but the dark wood was thick and tangled, and the ground was a treacherous mess of rocks and vines and fallen branches. They groped their way slowly, one foot at a time.

Bill said there were bears. Josh hoped they'd be hibernating by now, if there really were bears. Verna said no, but Verna didn't know anything.

You couldn't see a bear in the dark. It would see you first. Suppose you put your hand out, thinking it was a tree, and it was *fur?* He shivered.

"We'll never get to the highway," wailed Polly. "Josh, it's ten miles maybe."

"Not that far. Maybe three." But he didn't know. It might be ten.

"But it'll take us a week," she cried. "Just creeping along like this. We'll freeze to death!"

"We can't freeze to death if we keep moving. And if we just keep moving, even this slow, we've got to get there *some* time."

Inch by inch they stumbled on, groping and tripping like a nightmare-long game of pin-the-tail.

It wasn't completely dark, like being shut in a closet. The stars were a long way off, but stars are lights. Their eyes were used to the night by now, and they could see the thicker darkness of a tree trunk in front of them, and maybe even a bear if there was one. But they couldn't see prickers, or the junk underfoot. Josh banged his shin on a fallen tree and said some of Bill's bad words.

After a long time they heard a car.

"The highway!" cried Polly.

It wasn't, though. "It's over that way, the car," said Josh. "Beside us. It's the little road. It must be Bill coming back."

"Oh," said Polly, bitterly.

Josh thought of Bill and poor drunk, dumb Verna explaining that the kids were gone. What would he do? Go bursting out of the house, probably, staring around at the dark. Maybe he had a flashlight in the car.

But they were far and deep into the woods by now. He wouldn't find them with just a flashlight, and the whole woods to look in.

"Can't we walk on the road, now that he's back?" asked Polly.

"No. When he can't find us, he'll go driving back and forth on the road, looking."

"Oh. Yeah."

The only sounds now were the crunch of their feet in the leaves, and the snap of twigs and branches they stepped on, and the thin, mean whistle of the wind.

"Im *freezing*," said Polly. "My ears ache. I'll probably get pneumonia."

Josh tried to keep his spirits up by thinking about home—how warm it would be. No matter how late it was, even the middle of the night, his mother would fix him something hot to eat, and everyone would stay up in their bathrobes to hear all about it. Even his brother Steve would listen and ask questions. His father would clap him on the shoulder.

Home. Hot chocolate. Hot soup. A hot bath. His own bed.

He looked for Polaris, and then reached back to pull Polly by the sleeve. "We're too far this way," he said. "We have to go more left."

He stepped in a squelchy place, and icy water soaked into his shoe. Overhead the stars still hung in their proper places, cheering him on.

Polly tripped and fell sprawling into sharp rocks.

"Ow, my knee! My *knee!*" she cried. "I hit my knee! Ow, ow, *ow!*"

Josh felt around for her in the dark. "Get up," he said. "You can't just lie there. Come on, get up."

"I *can't.* I hurt my knee."

He took a handful of her jacket and pulled. "If you just lie there you'll freeze to death."

"I don't care. I can't walk any more. My knee hurts and I'm tired and I'm freezing, and I'm not going to walk any more." She huddled down in the darkness and began to cry. "You go on if you want," she sobbed.

Josh thought it might be nice to lie down and cry too. Just stay there crying and waiting in the woods until somebody else did something about them. After all, they were only kids. Somebody ought to take care of them.

But of course nobody would. Nobody in the whole world knew where they were, not even Bill and Verna. They would just die.

He gave Polly a great yank by the jacket. "Polly Conover, get up right this minute," he said fiercely. "Stop that stupid crying. Don't you see, we *have* to keep going? We *have to.* Get up and come on."

Polly gathered herself up in the dark and stood, wobbling, on her hurt knee. "I can feel it bleeding," she said, and sniffled.

"We'll go slow if it hurts. The only thing we can't do is just stop."

They crept on again, Polly limping and sniffling. After a while, she said sulkily, "I thought you were supposed to be so chicken."

Josh thought about that, trying to unhook a blackberry bush from his sleeve. "If we ever get home from here, I hope I never have to do anything brave again. Not even ride on the ferris wheel. It's just that sometimes there's things you've got to do anyway. Ouch." He had stabbed his finger on a pricker. He sucked it. Funny to be bleeding in the dark, invisibly. "You okay? Come on, then."

86

Inch by inch, they pushed their way through the tangled night woods. An owl flapped overhead, and then called, from a distance. The night and the woods went on and on, to the edge of the world, the edge of forever. It seemed as if morning must be coming, but it wasn't.

Their faces were so stiff with cold they felt like Hallowe'en masks. Josh's wet foot ached clear to the bone. They might have been stumbling and creeping forever through the same dark thicket without ever moving, like a bad dream.

Then, "There's a *light!*" cried Polly.

"Where?"

"Right there! Look! It's the highway!"

But the light stood still. They stared until their eyes watered and made rainbow-colored haloes around it.

It wasn't a car. It was a window. They edged closer.

There was a clearing in front of them, where a patch of bare sky showed beyond the three trunks. The prickers and vines were thicker here, the way they get at the edge of a clearing, because the sun shines in.

This was not what they'd been looking for. Not Route 200. It was a little square house in a clearing with a light on upstairs. They stood still, hesitating like deer.

"Listen," said Polly, and squeezed his arm fiercely. "Suppose it's the same house? Suppose we really did go around in a circle, like my dad said, and that's Bill and Verna in there?"

Suppose they had? It was the same kind of house. They would knock on the door, and Bill would reach out and grab them by the shoulders, and drag them inside, and tie them up with ropes.

No. Polaris burned over his right shoulder, just as it had all along. Besides, it wasn't really the same house.

They could see now that it was bigger and had bushes under the windows.

They pushed their way through the tangle at the edge of the woods and limped across the short frosty grass and up the steps.

Josh knocked on the front door, waited, and then knocked again harder.

From inside, they could hear footsteps on the stairs and a voice that seemed to be talking to itself. A downstairs light went on. "Now who do you suppose that could be?" asked the voice. "Somebody lost, most likely," it answered itself.

The door swung open and a tall old man stood there in the blazing light, peering kindly out at them. Not Bill. A white-haired man in a bathrobe, and behind him was a different, cozier room, with warm air rushing out from it, and lots of fat cozy chairs and the shape of a birdcage on a stand with a cover over it.

A gray cat slipped out between the man's ankles like a wisp of smoke. Josh reached down, gathered it up, and held it.

"Excuse me," he said. "I'm sorry to bother you like this. But we're the ones that got kidnapped."

chapter eleven

So none of it happened the way Josh had planned.

Instead of a highway, there was a house; and instead of his mother making cocoa, there was an old man making hot strong tea with lots of milk and sugar, and calling the police, and the cat, Smoky, wrapping itself around their legs and purring for milk.

The police said they would be there as quickly as possible, and someone would call the Blakes and Conovers to say the kids were free and safe.

The man's name was Mr. Baldwin. He washed Polly's knee and tied a piece of clean old sheet around it because he didn't have any Band-Aids. He put Josh's muddy shoe on a radiator to dry.

"And you came all that way in the woods," he kept saying. "Imagine that. That's a good piece of walking in the dark."

It was nice to be in a real house again, even if it wasn't his own. Nice to be with someone ordinary, someone who wasn't a crook.

The loud-ticking clock on the mantelpiece said it was a quarter of eleven. They had been in the woods since five-thirty.

Mr. Baldwin made them cheese sandwiches and took the cover off the birdcage so they could meet the parakeet. Its name was Richard, Mr. Baldwin said, and it was very old for a parakeet, but it had never learned to say anything at all, not even "hello."

"I got it to have a little something to talk to," said Mr. Baldwin. "For company. My wife died back in sixty-three, and after that I took to talking to myself. 'Think it'll clear up soon?' I'd say, and then I'd answer, 'Yeah, wind's out of the east, we ought to see a little sunshine by noon.' It made me feel like a fool. So I got a parakeet, but all it says is 'chirp.' Sometimes I say, 'chirp' to him, and he says 'chirp' back, and that's about as far as we get."

Polly and Josh were still leaning against the radiator soaking up the heat and eating their sandwiches when the police came.

They came in three cars with flashing lights. One car to take Josh and Polly in, and two to go catch Bill and Verna.

Josh told them how to find the little house. The two cars drove away quietly without the flashing lights, but Josh thought Bill and Verna would have to be even dumber than they were to still be hanging around.

"Boy, I hope they catch them," said Polly. "I hope they go to jail for a thousand years."

Josh wondered if they'd let Verna smoke in jail, and whether there was television. It was kind of sad to think about.

They said good-bye to Mr. Baldwin. He shook their hands.

"It's been a pleasure," he said. "Not much happens around here. Nice to have the excitement now and then.

And somebody to talk to that answers back."

They rode to the state police barracks out on the highway. It was warm and bright and busy, with cops coming and going and drinking coffee, and phones ringing. Josh and Polly had to answer a lot of questions. Then the police let them talk to their families on the phone. Everyone was too excited to make sense. Polly talked to her father, because her mother had had hysterics from relief, and the doctor had come to give her a shot to quiet her down.

Then there was the long drive home. Josh had forgotten how far they'd come. Of course, they went faster going back, because the police didn't have to obey the speed limit.

"Aren't you going to blow the siren?" asked Polly.

"We'd wake everyone up," said the cop who wasn't driving.

"There isn't anyone to wake up," said Polly. "Just woods and farms."

"We'd wake up the cows," said the cop. "It's bad for their milk." But he blew the siren anyway, just for half a mile or so. Josh and Polly felt very grand, speeding through the night with the light flashing and the siren howling. It was terribly noisy though, and Josh was glad when they turned it off.

"I wonder if my dad'll be mad about the fishing rod," said Polly. "He gets pretty mad sometimes, if I lose something that costs a lot."

"I bet he won't," said Josh.

They listened to the calls on the police radio, and that was exciting, except there wasn't much happening at that time of night. A truck had turned over on a highway outside of Harrisburg. Somebody had had a heart attack, and the police ambulance was taking him to the hospital. There was a fight in a bar somewhere, and somebody got stabbed with a knife.

Polly said, "I'm going to be a policeman when I grow up."

"I'm not," said Josh.

The cops had some candy bars and shared them with Josh and Polly.

The night rushed past the speeding car.

It was after four o'clock in the morning when they got home, but everyone was awake and all the lights were on in Josh's house, which was where they went first.

"See you," he said to Polly. He was just thanking the cops when everyone came pouring out to meet him.

There never was such hugging and laughing and patting and chattering, with everyone talking at once. Even his brother Steve, who never said much, said, "Hey, it's nice you're back."

There he was in his own kitchen again with everything the same as if he'd never been gone, and the lights all blazing away in the middle of the night. His little cat rubbed against his legs and arched her back to be patted.

His mother took a good look at him in the bright kitchen light and sent him up to take a bath before he did another thing.

"And if you can't get clean by yourself," she said, "and I mean your neck, and ears, and *everything*, then I'm coming up to scrub you myself."

She always said that.

The hot water felt good. He was pretty crusty all over, and he actually did do some washing, and then just lay and soaked and looked at the ceiling for a long time. He would have stayed even longer, only some more police had come, and he had to get out and put on his pajamas and bathrobe and talk to them.

These two were the detective kind that don't wear uniforms, and they were more serious and important than the others. They said that Bill and Verna were gone from the little house, and nobody had found them yet.

The detectives wrote down everything Josh said, which made him feel about eight feet tall. He told them what Bill and Verna looked like and wore, and the kind of car they had, and that they didn't have much money or any gun any more.

"So you disarmed them single-handed," said one officer solemnly. "Thank you. That's a big help."

Josh felt pretty good.

They called the holdup at the country store "armed robbery." That made it sound more important than it was, but Josh didn't know how to explain that it wasn't like that. Armed robbery sounded like swarms of bank robbers with machine guns. Not just Bill with a big clumsy shotgun getting cigarettes for Verna, and Josh grabbing crackers and lima beans.

All the police made Bill and Verna sound more important than they really were. It seemed like too much fuss to make over Bill with his bald spot and his crumpled-up suit, and Verna chewing gum and watching television. On the other hand, Josh didn't know any other crooks, not personally, and maybe they were all like that.

When the detectives left it was morning, and they turned off the lights. Josh's mother made a huge breakfast for the whole family. She made pancakes, and Josh ate eleven. Steve ate fourteen. She cooked a whole package of bacon, and there was orange juice and milk, and Josh finished off with a bowl of Rice Krispies and an apple. He was stuffed. It felt good.

Nobody said anything about going to work or school. They just sat around the table and talked. Josh's little cat jumped up and walked delicately among the syrupy plates, looking for bacon crumbs, but this was such a special occasion that nobody pushed her off.

Then Mr. Conover came over with an enormous package.

"Young man," he said to Josh, "I'd like to shake your hand."

To Josh's father, he said, "Stanley, I hope you realize what this youngster did. Just saved my daughter's life, that's all. Just about the bravest thing *I* ever heard of, that's all."

Josh was embarrassed. "I didn't save her *life*, exactly. I mean, they weren't going to hurt us—I don't think. They weren't even mean to us much."

"Just saved her *life*," said Mr. Conover. "Just stood up to a couple of vicious criminals and got her out of there and took her through the woods to safety. In the night. That's all. Just found his way by the *stars*, she tells me. Young man, you're going to be a lot of help to me on the boat I'm getting. Navigating—like Columbus."

"Thank you," said Josh. His ears felt hot. He was too polite to say that Columbus was about as lost as a person can possibly get. He thought he was in *India*, for heaven's sake.

"You know what a young man like that deserves, Stanley? He deserves just about the finest telescope money can buy, that's what." And Mr. Conover handed Josh the big package and bowed.

94

The box said "J. L. Cruze, Specializing in Optics." Josh opened the flaps and reached in, and drew it part-way out. It was big. It was much better than Polly's. It wasn't a toy at all. With a telescope like that, you could see anything. The craters on the moon and the spiral galaxy north of Andromeda. The stars in the great square of Pegasus.

"Now wait a minute, Harold," said Josh's father. "I'm afraid he's a little young for an instrument like that."

Josh hung his head.

"A youngster that can do what this one did isn't too young for *anything*," said Mr. Conover firmly. "And I do believe he saved our Polly. Who knows what would have happened next, if they hadn't gotten out of there?"

"Well," said Josh's mother doubtfully, looking at the telescope.

Josh was embarrassed, and tried to hide his face, bending down over the beautiful telescope.

A telescope like that would be almost like traveling in the stars, seeing them up so close. It would be as good as having a spaceship. Better, because you could stay home. Safe at home.

And then, crouched over like that, sleep came washing over him. He was so sleepy his eyelids seemed to swell up and sag down over his eyes. He couldn't lift them. He couldn't pick his head up. He felt as if he were melting, and stars were swimming around him. He was almost clear asleep.

Because, after all, he was only a boy, and he was home, and he had been up the whole night long, and now he heard his mother saying, "Stanley, all that can wait. It's time this hero went to bed."

ABOUT THE AUTHOR

Barbara Holland was born in Washington, D.C., and lived for many years in Philadelphia, where she worked as an advertising copywriter and wrote magazine stories. Recently she moved to the tiny country village of Birchrunville, Pennsylvania, where she now lives with her husband, her 16-year-old daughter, 11-year-old twin sons, and a variety of animals. *Prisoners at the Kitchen Table* was written as a Christmas present for her sons, and is her first book for Clarion.